# *Culture*
# *Clock*

# *Culture Clock*

A Novel Written in
Lockdown, After
Zoom Meetings
(and sometimes during)

**Bo Bestvina**

Paperback ISBN: 979-8218-70575-6
Library of Congress Number: 2025912103
First paperback edition: 2025
Edited by Sage Santiago
Cover art by Devon Morris
Layout by Andrea Reider

Printed in the USA by Village Books.
1200 11th St, Bellingham, WA 98225
https://www.villagebooks.com/

# Dedication

To my brother Michael, a fellow writer and thinker. You would entertain any idea, even those I was more interested in. To Luke, for giving me a five-dollar kit on writing your first novel. You found the thing I needed to weather that era of my life. To Rhonda, for thoroughly reading my first draft and telling me what worked and what didn't. To my editor, Sage, for asking for more descriptive writing. To Robin, for nurturing creativity and encouraging with love. To her uncle Howard for telling me "if you want to pitch this book as a movie, you gotta publish it first."

# Contents

# *Authors Note*

In the middle of COVID, I was living in an unused Zen Buddhist center in Seattle, rent-free. They needed someone to watch over the place in case someone tried to break in. My "apartment" was the meditation space, a 30 by 30 ft. room with beautiful hardwood floors. I put my bed along one wall, and a foldup cot in the middle of the room. The cot is where the idea for this book came to me. Despite what the news was saying around the country, it seemed like a fair amount of people in Seattle weren't bothered by COVID, because they were young, affluent tech workers who could order all their food to their door. Living in Seattle made me wonder, "what if everyone in the world lived as coders, and humanity just did away with traditions and community?"

I was also teaching middle school at the time, on a zoom screen in the zen center kitchen. A new kid came to school one day. He was hilarious and he kept an open mind. He gave me hope that we may get to keep a relational world even when we are having coffee with AI holograms (you'll read about them later in the book).

This book was written in the space of a pause for billions of people around the world. Many other novels were written during this time as well. It seems like pausing helps many people focus back on the bigger picture of what to do with their lives.

# 1

## *Familiar Faces*

The sunset over the hills to the west reflected off of the few tall apartment buildings in Quelter. The whole town continued to radiate the warmth of the day—warmth that energized couples and groups meandering their way to dinner, who harnessed the time to clarify their thoughts as they talked. The residents had chosen to live this way. They had accepted the consequences of denying the evolution, speed, and efficiency of the rest of the world.

Quelter Valley, flat as a pancake, wore shades of green and brown depending on where farmers were in their crop cycle. Some crops gave Quelter an income, while others fed the town through farmers' markets—a cute, yet antiquated concept by modern world standards. Farmland gave way to great plant diversity in the hills to the west, where Bunchgrass, Sagebrush, Hemlock, Indian Paintbrush, Balsamroot, and Lupines gripped the dry earth.

Vic and Gale held hands on their way to Tammy's restaurant. They didn't say much because, at times, they both felt as if they'd already said everything they could in their thirty-five years together. Yet they were comfortable; they knew the precious commodity of silence could not be marketed and therefore existed outside the boundaries of popular culture, which blasted its speakers in every part of the world except within the communities that intentionally resisted it.

The first star in the night shone over the dark blue horizon. "Make a wish," said Gale.

Vic thought for a minute, as if his wish could actually come true. "I wish to have some kind of lasting impact on the world," he said.

"Oh Vic, get over it. We both know you've made an impact. Make a better wish than that," replied Gale.

"Okay, I wish to give away some wisdom to all the young know-it-alls these days, in exchange for back pain relief."

Gale smiled. "Much better. I wish we could live in the cabin in Sandbush within a year." She dreamed of leaving their turtle-paced town for a slug-paced retirement in a cabin in the mountains.

Vic wore a fedora and a button-up plaid shirt with jeans. His jeans were straight-cut to make him look taller than his 5'5" height. White hair, accented by his tan skin, shined below the sides of the fedora. His face, clean-shaven, had tight skin; while it made him look younger, it also made him look incomplete, as if the years slowed down to wait for some monumental challenge to be overcome or accepted.

Gale wore a green dress with yellow flowers on it and a light white jacket. When they went out, she wore her flat shoes. She didn't like the pressure to feel shorter than she was just to accommodate Vic's desire to feel taller than he was. She thought about ways to bring the issue up, but doing so could shine the light on other inequalities in the relationship.

They arrived at Tammy's at 6:30. The restaurant was seat-yourself-style, but it still had waiters and cooks, attracting tourists who wanted a glimpse into the past. They sat in a booth with tall back pads attached to solid oak. The couple looked at the same pictures they always looked at: one of the restaurant's opening two years back, in 2110, and another of the restaurant's waiters and cooks on a rafting trip.

Chad, their waiter, came by for drink orders.

Vic spoke first. "Hey Chad, I'll get a coffee with lots of creamers, as usual."

"I'll get a glass of merlot," said Gale.

While Gale looked at her menu, Vic stared down at the soft yellow light reflecting off the amber coating the dark wood table.

"Well, aren't you gonna look at your menu?" Gale asked.

"What's the use? I always get one of three things. You know that. I'll probably have the BLT tonight."

Gale sighed, hoping he'd order something healthier.

"Do you remember that time Casey stayed at our house and did the stand-up routine in the backyard?" asked Vic.

"How could I forget? He showed so much potential."

"He sure did, but that's not who I want to talk about. There was this guy in the audience of that party, he's been showing up in my dreams a lot lately. This unsuspecting guy with black hair, a chiseled face, a mole on his right cheek, a clean shave, a black hooded jacket, and dark blue jeans."

Gale looked impressed. "Wow, you remembered him that specifically, huh?"

"Yeah, but I can't recall his name."

"I think it was 'Wyoming'. Casey introduced us, and that name stuck with me."

Before Vic could go on, Chad returned. "Are you two ready to order?"

"Yeah, I'll get the Double Burger," said Vic.

"I thought you were getting the BLT?"

"Changed my mind."

"Okay, I'll get the Bacon Avocado Wrap, without the avocado. I mean, without the bacon," said Gale.

"Great! I'll just take those menus from you. Oh, and I'll go get your drinks. I've been spacy all day today. Sorry about that."

Vic gave Chad a parent's look. "Chad, you've been here at Tammy's for seven years. Ever think about finishing that art degree you started a while ago?"

"Yeah, I think about it all the time. It's honestly the fantasy that gets me through the days at this place. But we've got to wait for Ricky to be a little older for me to go back to school."

"Gotcha. You've got our support, Chad."

"Thanks Vic."

Vic turned back to Gale and took off his fedora. Taking off the hat meant he felt comfortable allowing the sheen of his bald head to shine like a lighthouse. "As I was saying, this guy at Casey's gig, he keeps showing up in my dreams with some new message. In one dream he reminded me of the time I gave a client bad advice and he left his family. He said as a therapist, I just dragged people's problems on. They were in a bag of trash, but instead of throwing them out, I ripped the bag and let them spill out all over the ground. Then he told me that college years represented a span of authenticity lost in later adulthood. That's when I had the meaning of life really figured out, studying whatever was interesting and spending late nights with the band. Guess he has a point. Then he shows up, pointing to this clock tower. 'Go to the clock tower,' he says."

The story piqued Gale's interest. She tucked her shoulder-length brown and gray hair behind her ears, then put her right elbow on the table and rested her head on her palm.

Vic went on. "Every time I get close, the clock tower slides back a little, as if it's not firmly attached to the earth."

"Have you thought about asking Casey who this guy is? I wonder what he does in real life," Gale asked.

"I bet he works in an office in Derise's clock tower." Derise, the big city over the mountain pass to the west of Quelter, kept the massive clock tower up as an homage to the past. At least that's what the city council told the public. In truth, companies in the city liked their employees to be reminded that time is of the essence when pursuing wealth and status.

"Okay, here is your Avocado Wrap, and here is the Double Burger. Can I get you guys anything else?"

"More coffee please," requested Vic.

Just then, a group of fifteen men and women dressed in professional clothing walked into the nearly empty restaurant. The leader of the pack asked the waiter if he could put some tables together, and requested if they could sit far away from the two old couples occupying the restaurant.

"Wonder what they're doing here," asked Gale.

"Oh, probably just planning to build a top-secret virology lab here in town," replied Vic, half-jokingly.

Gale didn't laugh. "Yeah, well, I'd be happy if they took all the squirrels getting into our garbage and tested their drugs on them."

At the far end of the restaurant, the group sat and began discussing how they'd launch their project.

"You do know many of the participants are going to want to leave in a week."

"Yes, but this is why it is crucial for us to build a sense of community among them. They have to feel like what they'll get at Culture Lab is better than anything they can find out there in the real world."

"The rainforest trip will be fun. Going on an adventure with total strangers, without technology, will feel like going to another planet."

They discussed their plans for the lab in Quelter—not a virology lab, though; they were calling it "Culture Lab."

"I don't know what Sonata is thinking with this. You can't just create a new culture overnight. It takes many years and isolation from other groups, which is impossible these days…"

Another group member interrupted. "Sonata is a visionary. She sees the only path to change is to unplug."

"And yet she ironically runs the biggest tech company on Earth."

"Be that as it may, look at what she wrote in the vision of her Master Plan: 'There is a blurred line between online identity and physical identity, and people are lost in it all, living without any continuity with the past. They're lost in this spin cycle of revising and reframing identity to find it's place in a rapidly changing world.'"

The leader jumped to get everyone back on track. "We can discuss the merits of Culture Lab another time. We are here to make sure everything is running smoothly. So first, is the facility ready?"

"Yes, but it's really just a house. We can stop calling it a facility. We added an extension because we didn't think it was quite enough space for fifty people."

"And the town people, are they asking a lot of questions?"

"No, we told them it's a retreat center for corporate teams. But they wouldn't be coming into Quelter unless it's an emergency. People calmed down knowing that."

"How do they feel about us being here, researching the town?"

"They felt fine after all getting 5K from Sonata."

Meanwhile, Vic and Gale enjoyed their dinner, mostly.

"This Double Burger makes my chest hurt," Vic complained.

"You always say that. Why don't you stop ordering it?"

"I wish you'd remind me."

"Want me to remind you to also drive on the right side of the road?" Gale knew she hit a nerve.

Vic didn't reply because he knew whatever reply came out would sting. He grabbed his black fedora and put it on. Then he stared at the large talking group. "I wonder if they are planning to build some new warehouse here."

Just then, one of the Culture Lab group members stood up and yelled:

"This whole idea is not even about creating culture. It is about creating desire. You all just want to restore people to this natural state so you can give Soradin even more pure data to develop garbage to sell them. I quit."

"Please don't go, Wyoming. We need you."

"I think you all just need to sit with your conscience for a while."

As Wyoming stormed out, Vic couldn't help but notice he looked an awful lot like the guy from his dreams. More formal clothes, but everything else was the same. Thick black hair, clean-shaven, chiseled face. Wyoming winked at the couple before leaving.

Vic stared at the glass door closing behind Wyoming. "I need to see if that's the guy from the party." He grabbed his jacket and slid out of the booth. When he got out to the parking lot, he saw Wyoming walking to his car. In an instant, the scene changed. Instead of a parking lot, Vic stood in a grassland savanna. Fifty meters away, he noticed a tribe of people in loin cloths gathered around a fire. But everything was frozen in time, including the flames of the fire. Everything was still except for Wyoming, who walked away from Vic while running his fingers through the tall, golden grass.

Vic rubbed his eyes and then started to see Wyoming disappear. It looked like an old camera took the picture, because the character in motion was fading. Vic rubbed his eyes again and opened them to see the parking lot.

"What the heck?" He wondered if he was experiencing hallucinations or schizophrenia. *Never heard of late-onset. What else could this be? Who were those people he was with?*

Vic reentered the restaurant with a confused look on his face and sat next to Gale.

"You look like you saw a ghost," she noted.

Vic wasn't sure how to explain what he saw.

"Um, no, not a ghost. I think it was Wyoming, but he got in his car so fast, I didn't get a chance to talk to him."

## 2

# *Saving Memories*

Noah had been working on the Culture Lab project in Quelter for two years when Wyoming went missing. As a Cultural Anthropologist, his job was to predict what would happen when the new cultures would be introduced to the town. As the rest of the world kept moving faster, Quelter stayed relatively in the past. They worked hard to keep their lives free of the identity chasms created by the rapidly changing expectations of the outside world. Soradin hoped Quelter's people would be more curious about new cultures simply because they weren't so preoccupied trying to recreate their identities.

Despite meeting and interviewing many people throughout town, Noah struggled to build any real friendships in Quelter. He wondered if townies just didn't trust outsiders, or if he had closed himself off to close relationships since his divorce.

One way to free himself from ruminating on things was to go on long bike rides on country roads around town. Two days after Wyoming went missing, Noah was on one of his rides when he heard his cell phone vibrating inside the bike bag. He pulled his bike into a gravel pull-off to take the call.

"Hey Noah, it's Tim. Did you finish the beliefs and traditions report on Quelter?"

"Yeah, I was meaning to send that to you this afternoon. Pretty much what we expected: people holding on—churches, diners, small talk, family farms—vestiges of culture from long ago."

"Excellent," replied Tim. "Say, can you ask around about Wyoming? He'd been staying in town for about a month before he went missing, so I am curious if any locals know anything about his disappearance."

"Sure," replied Noah. "I guess it is possible someone met him at a café or bar. But we both know Wyoming wanted to leave Soradin for years. I just never thought his exit would be so dramatic."

Before Wyoming left his human body that night in the parking lot, he'd worked in accounting at Soradin. He worked his way up over the years, but only for the money. He got to a point where he didn't need the money anymore and started showing signs of boredom. In an era of over-stimulation, when employers encouraged employees two hours of social media consumption and two hours of online gaming per day, boredom became a serious concern. Boredom could result in too much imagination, which left untreated could cause someone to lose their loyalty to the core values of the world's dominant culture: comfort, security, and entertainment. So, as Soradin noticed Wyoming's boredom, they persuaded him to join the Culture Lab team.

After knocking on doors and talking to people all afternoon—people who had small town charm masking their distaste of newcomers—Noah decided to head home. On his way back to his car, he noticed a beautiful piece of spiraling brass metal hanging from the burgundy-colored trim on someone's front porch.

He walked up to the second step below the porch to get a closer look. "Haven't seen one of those in twenty years," he said to himself.

Just then, the door opened, and a women in her mid 60s with fluffy red hair and wearing a peach-colored blouse stepped out.

"Originally, tribal people built wood ones meant to distract someone in distress," she said.

"Oh, hey Barbara. Sorry, I didn't realize you lived here."

"Oh, so you were instead just stalking someone you didn't know?" she replied jokingly.

Noah didn't get it. "Uh, no. I've just been going around town, asking people if they knew Wyoming. He worked for Soradin and went missing the other day."

"Oh yes, I heard about that and saw a picture of him online. I am just about to finish making dinner. Would you like to join me?"

Noah froze. He'd only met Barbara once before at the grocery store. She was twice his age, but he knew she was single and he had no other plans. He looked to the left of the porch, at the birch tree in her front yard. The tree seemed to bring the darkening blue sky behind it closer to Earth.

"Yeah, sure, why not," he said.

The living room he entered looked different than any room he'd seen in a long time; it displayed cultural artifacts instead of modern art or plants. On the mantle he saw a bronze Chimera statue from ancient China, a cracked Anasazi jar, a picture of Barbara with her husband, and other photos of her family. He sat on her old couch, with cushion covers of intersecting brown and gray yarn that had dulled with age. He smelled lasagna, cinnamon, potpourri, and the unique scent released by opening an old book, all at once.

Barbara checked on dinner and then sat in her blue recliner across from him. She started with an unsolicited story. "Not too long ago I worked for an organization called Saving Memories. It was kind of my retirement gig. This group went around collecting toys people were planning to throw away—trucks, fake guns, dolls, and so on. Artifacts like these were getting tossed by the millions over the years, since screens had replaced them. So a group of crazy people with nothing better to do started categorizing this stuff in an old warehouse."

Noah looked interested but a bit confused. "So what does this all have to do with Wyoming?"

"When I saw the 'Wyoming's Missing' announcement, I was immediately thrown back to my time working for Saving Memories, when I had these dreams about someone who looked a lot like Wyoming. When I told co-workers about him, they admitted someone who looked like that was coming into their dreams, too."

Noah rubbed the light brown patch of hair below his lower lip. "Interesting, what do you think he was trying to tell you?"

"Well, he would bring me back into periods of my life, like when I first met my husband. Those were good times, like the time my husband found out I liked lasagna and made me the best lasagna on the third Friday of every month that we were married. So it was neat to get those kinds of dreams. But the guy also showed me the times I messed up big. Like when I lied to my husband and daughter and told them I was going to Argentina to collect some rare artifacts, but instead I went to Vegas with my girlfriends. When my credit card got canceled in Vegas, I had to call my husband for money, which was humiliating."

"Did the guy ever show you your future, or just your past?"

"Sometimes he pointed to this clock tower. Friends at work got the same dream. I don't know if he was saying time is running out in my life, or if the answer to some of life's problems is just time. Or maybe something else. Would you excuse me for a bit?"

Barbara walked to the kitchen to check her lasagna. She always made enough for two and threw out the half she didn't eat even though she could have saved it. She then stood in the opening between the living room and the kitchen.

"Okay, you can wash up in the bathroom down the hall," she directed Noah, as if he were her grandchild. Being outside of any family role at this stage in life, Noah obediently got up and looked to her for further instructions.

"Down the hall and to your left," she said.

The bathroom had green walls, a white vanity, and framed picture of a cat on its back. A dark green curtain hid the mold growing on the bottom edge of the shower. Curiosity won, and Noah peeled back the curtain. Instead of the anticipated stained white tub with a non-slip bath mat, he saw a pile of sentimental knick-knacks, trophies, and awards. The drain had rust around it, and Noah wondered why Barbara was hoarding some of this stuff and where she was showering.

One trophy read, "Jack, Our Family's All-Star." Another bore, "Riley, Premier Girls Soccer #3, State." Then there was a little handheld book with a red cover and an elastic band wrapped around it. Noah opened the cover:

*Dear Dalton, in this book you will find a list of countries your mom and I visited before you were born. For each culture, you will find out how the people spoke to men and women, the elderly, and strangers. You will also see expressions they found offensive, gestures of kindness, and popular superstitions. Hold on to this book Dalton, for many things will have changed by the time you are my age.*

*Love, Dad*

Noah had three options at this point: 1) Leave the book, pretend he never saw it 2) Bring the book out and ask Barbara about it, hoping she wouldn't scold him for looking in her shower 3) Take the book, say nothing, eat dinner, and leave. He considered options two and three.

"Everything okay in there?" Barbara asked.

Noah hesitated before responding, "Yeah, just finishing up."

He put the little book in his pocket, but it stuck out a bit. *If she asks, just tell her it's the book you use to take notes on any information people have on Wyoming,* he thought.

He sat at the kitchen table. "Wow this looks great, Barb, thank you."

"You know, you kind of look like him," she replied. "When he was younger, I suppose."

Noah knew Barb was talking about her deceased husband, but didn't feel like going down that road. And yet, he didn't have any good ideas on how to pivot the conversation, so the two spent a little time in silence.

Barb broke the silence. "So how have you been liking your time in Quelter?"

"The people are friendly. It's fine, I guess. It's hard to make friends though. To a town clung to tradition, a divorced person may as well have a contagious disease."

"When my husband died, I felt that way too. During our time together, I did not notice what type of social capital the marriage provided. After he died, I got pretty lonely and started looking for things to shift my attention to. That's when I found Saving Memories, and it became my focus to discover the simple joy of toys and how they could find their way back to kids."

Noah pulled out the little red book and put it on the table. "I took something from you, Barb. It's this book here. I took it from your bathroom, and I was planning on not telling you, but now I can't stand not to tell you."

"Oh yes, Dalton's little book of cultures. Keep it." Noah gave a half smile, the sincere kind. "That book may give your life a whole new direction, Noah. It's like a travel guide, written by a couple around fifty years ago, in a ten-year period known as the 'Earth's Blanket.'"

Noah pushed his upper lip up with his lower lip to show intrigue. "I think I read about that somewhere. Why is it called that?"

"Because during that time, corporations provided tech jobs to the last people living in abject poverty. In other words, no one on the planet would be cold or hungry again."

"Wow. Can't believe I know so little about this."

Barb went on. "The last cultural traditions and rituals were also performed in this period—the last Chinese New Year, the last Christmas, the last Bar Mitzva, and so on. Actually, my family had one of the last Christmas celebrations. Mom made ham and mashed potatoes, and we all decorated a real Christmas tree. My parents invited a lot of people, but just one of my uncles came. Everyone else said, 'it's just too inconvenient with everything going on at work, but maybe next year.' Well, that was the last year we celebrated the holiday. I still have the little stuffed giraffe mom gave me, but the family threw away the rest of the toys the following year."

Noah looked puzzled. "What an experience. So everyone just naturally stopped celebrating holidays?"

"Sadly, yes. The few who protested the demise of such traditions wrote fascinating books and articles and even a few movies, and people found such works of art to be heart-warming but not much more."

"I just... don't get it," replied Noah.

"Sweetie," said Barb, in the tone she'd have when talking with a child. "People just found tradition to be inconvenient— something unnecessary, especially as most gifts became digital. There was nothing to be opened, so the whole thing got boring. Devoutly religious Christians held on a little longer, but eventually they succumbed to the apparent ease of life without ritual."

"Wow. Does this book have some of the last non-English languages in it, too?"

"Yep, the couple recorded a hundred words from each of the three last non-English languages around. All the speakers of those languages have since passed away."

They shared a grieving silence before Noah changed the subject to something lighter. "So, you ever go to the bowling alley in town?" He really didn't care if she had gone to the bowling alley, but didn't know what else to ask.

The conversation went back and forth from trivial to monumental for another hour or so. Before leaving, Noah gave Barb a hug. While there were still so many questions about Earth's Blanket, and Wyoming, Noah felt alright not resolving them. The sense of mystery, in fact, made him feel his heartbeat again.

As Noah walked home, a satellite streamed across the sky, reminding him how quickly opportunities could come to pass. So he pulled out the little book to Dalton and read it with the respect a historian would read an ancient scroll.

3

# *A Strange Calling*

Vic never mentioned what he'd actually seen that night in the parking lot of the restaurant. The idea of researching abnormal visions in old age tempted him, but he just wanted one flashlight in this mysterious cave, not many. So instead he spent some time contemplating the memory of the parking lot turning into a grassland and Wyoming walking away from him. He wanted to see what could well up from his subconscious.

Three days after Wyoming went missing, Vic had the most unusual dream. At half his age (32), he boarded a flight from Quelter to Simone, about 300 miles away, to see his mother. He always drove this route in real life, but the dream put him in a small Cessna plane with the words "Soradin Unites the World," stenciled on the side in black. He landed in Simone at nine o'clock, but the town was darker than normal. At the tarmac, Vic picked up a rental car by just getting in and going. He headed to his mom's house across the river that snaked through the middle of the town.

On his way to the bridge, Vic noticed street lights were on but no cars were on the road. Everyone was inside on

19

devices—computers, phones, VR, etc. He wondered if Soradin told them, implicitly through social media ads, that night time wasn't safe. It was much safer to stay inside and entertained in a virtual world tailored perfectly to one's desires without any sense of risk or time.

When he got to the bridge, a posted sign read, "This bridge has structure issues and will be closed until further notice. Do not attempt to cross, even by foot."

Vic got out of his car and started walking across the middle of the bridge. The moon behind moving clouds cast a little light on the bridge and one side of the wide river's sheen below. As he walked across the bridge, a face appeared in the light gray clouds above.

"Hello Vic," the face said in a deep, gentle voice.

"Wow, you look just like that man I saw the other night, the one who turned my world upside down. Where did you go? What was all that?"

"I am Wyoming," said the face in the clouds. "The body I used is at rest in a place hard to find. And the scene of early humans… well that's just something for you to think about. That's where humanity could head if they don't…"

"Don't what?"

"Don't… Nevermind that now, Vic. I have an important mission for you."

"A—a mission?"

"Vic, do you remember the time your grandma sat you down and told you the story of her dollhouse, equipped with miniature sewing machine, piano, secretary desk, and China set?"

"Sure do. That little house even had a loft, where her dolls, Ruth and Esther, would talk late into the night. Grandma said that loft was a place for her dolls to dream big together. She always had her own big dreams but no one to share them with, so she played them out with her dolls."

Wyoming disappeared for a few seconds, then reappeared in the cloud. "Vic, that dollhouse is the reason you became a therapist. The story of that dollhouse gave you a sense of where you came from, and people looked to you because they lost that sense in themselves."

Vic continued to go along, although he began to sense it was a dream. "Yeah, I think those dolls ultimately motivated Grandma to become a pilot and tour guide, to follow what she loved. I look to her spirit when I am confused about a certain direction."

"Good, you may need her spirit to make sense of the direction I am about to put you on. Vic, I want you to figure out how to recreate your grandma's dollhouse, with the miniature piano and all. I'd like you to create many of them and sell them to people around the world. When you wake up, you will have ten million dollars in your bank account, gifted to you by a millionaire friend of mine. I want you to use that money to start a company building dollhouses like your grandma's."

Vic wanted to ask about the millionaire friend but had a better question. "Dollhouses? That's gonna save the world?"

"No, but it could save the human spirit."

Wyoming waved goodbye in the clouds, which then rolled away. Vic looked straight ahead. He was high above the water on a suspension cable bridge. There were construction materials scattered along the side walkway—pieces of scaffolding and pink ribbon. The bridge seemed to disappear in the distance, as if whatever was on the other side didn't matter.

Vic woke up and went straight to the computer. At midnight, a deposit of ten million dollars had been wire transferred to his bank account from Andiste Swoft's account. He tried to look up the giver's personal information, a social media account or phone number, but found nothing.

# 4

# *Why Dollhouses?*

After seeing that deposit on his computer, that unexplainable blessing and burden, Vic went down into the basement to find the dollhouse he'd inherited from his grandmother. It was still there, wrapped in plastic and set on some boxes behind his bandsaw. "I'll get you in the morning," he said to himself.

Instead of trying to go back to sleep, Vic decided to take a walk. He grabbed his fedora, jacket, and dog leash, then he called his black lab, Jasper, and watched the old dog rise slowly. But as soon as he stood up, he decided to lay back down. So Vic went on his own.

The lock on the front door was stuck shut, and Vic went out the back. *We really outta fix that ol' lock,* he thought.

On the walk, Vic wondered for a bit if he were losing his mind, but his footsteps, the brisk air, and the moon peaking through the clouds assured him of normal sensation and perception. So he turned his thoughts to his task.

*Why dollhouses?*

That's when he ran into Noah, who walked regularly in the middle of the night, for no other reason than to think. He knew Vic from conversations at the grocery store.

"Hey, Vic, what are you doing out this late?"

"Oh well, I was just… well I guess I'll just tell you the truth. I was just told in a dream that I would have ten million dollars in my bank when I awoke, and it came true."

Noah stopped walking and turned to Vic. "What? Are you serious?"

"Afraid I am. Hey, do you want it?"

"Wait, you don't want it?" Noah replied.

"Well, keeping it means I'd have to use the money to make replicas of my grandmother's childhood dollhouse, potentially thousands of them. I am not sure I want to do that."

"You know, Vic, I wouldn't normally believe you, but something strange happened to me this evening as well."

Vic's firm brow released its tension, and he let out a sigh. "What happened?"

"Well, I got this little red book—actually, I stole it—from Barbara Hunsacker. I take it you know her?"

"Oh yeah, Barb and I go way back. Tell me about this book."

"Well, I saw it in her tub, along with all this other junk she kept from this project called Saving Memories."

"Oh yeah, I know about Saving Memories. So she hoarded some things from there? Not surprised with Barb. Once she lost her husband, she took to hoarding."

Noah honored the space Vic created to think about Barbara's life. "Yeah, that's too bad, what she went through." Right after he said it, he thought of his ex-wife Heidi. He thought about calling her just to "check in."

"What was in the little red book?" asked Vic.

"It has a encyclopedia of extinct cultures, you could say, documented by a couple who gave it to their son, who then grew up and donated it to Saving Memories. It has detailed observations of family and community traditions, norms, dress, types of housing and architecture, and even other languages."

"So you found some travelers' log. Why is that so special?" asked Vic.

"Vic, I gotta confess something to you. I've been in Quelter for two years trying to understand the culture here. It's all part of this project Soradin is conducting called Culture Lab. They plan to grow cultures from the ground up."

"Let me me stop ya. Grow cultures? Like yogurt?"

"Not exactly, but there is a funny similarity. When you make yogurt you add probiotic bacteria to milk and let it multiply. Soradin is working to create new cultures and multiply the beliefs and traditions of these cultures around the world. The idea is to take willing participants and de-culturalize them over a few years and then release them back into the population."

"Wouldn't they just revert back to the culture dominating the entire planet now?" asked Vic.

"We are working to ensure that won't happen. Soradin is planning to market these new cultures, and the products they create, and present them as yet another novelty to keep people entertained."

Vic tried connecting the dots. "So you're interested in the book so you can have other groups of people to compare us small town hillbillies to?"

"You are fascinating hillbillies, if that makes you feel better," joked Noah.

Vic felt flattered, as if the comment was directed right at him, and not at Quelter in general.

"But seriously, this is a firsthand account of extinct cultures, and it's a hand-written source. You can't get any better than that…"

"Let me see the book," asked Vic. He put out his hand, expecting Noah to agree. Noah looked at him for a second and handed it over. The book was only three by five inches. The pages were thick and cream-colored.

Vic thumbed through the pages under the light from a street light. Then he stopped at a page titled "Meal-time Traditions" and read part of the journal entry aloud:

"We were in a remote village in northern India where people ate rice and curry with their hands. According to them, touching the food was an important part of the eating experience."

"Would have been nice to visit a place like *that*," Vic commented. He handed the book back to Noah.

Just then, a comet flared through the sky. It made the two reflect on all the cultures that have come and gone under the stars.

Noah started, "I don't want to say I wish it hit the earth but…"

"But you want people to feel some kind of shake at their core," finished Vic.

Noah sighed. "Yeah, I do."

Instead of making a wish, Vic made an offer. "So you got this book, which I am sure Soradin would love to get their hands on, and I've got this money I am supposed to build a bunch of dollhouses with—"

Noah cut him off. "Right, let's get back to the dollhouses."

"Thanks. Wyoming, that guy who went missing, showed up in my dream and put me on this mission to build dollhouses. He reminded me of the story my grandmother told me about this dollhouse. He said I should make thousands like it."

"And you woke up and checked your bank account and the money was actually there?"

"Yep."

"Wild."

"Wyoming manifested as a cloud in my dream with the same facial features as the guy in real life—chiseled face and a black sole patch of hair under his lip. I didn't know what to make of it. Tonight he showed up and told me to make all these dollhouses with the ten million that would just mysteriously appear in my bank account."

Noah rubbed his sole patch. "What an unusual calling."

Vic nodded, then vocalized his nostalgia. "I loved my grandma's stories about that dollhouse—about her imagination running through each meticulously arranged room. She'd even sew mini blue curtains for the living room, and mini white lace placemats for the mini dining room table. That house gave her a place to develop her imagination, and indeed her identity. We've lost that imagination and wonder somehow since then."

"What if we didn't just build her dollhouse, but others based on the cultures in Dalton's book?" Noah proposed. "Look, Dalton's parents drew examples of the housing styles in all the cultures they visited."

Vic smiled. "That's much more interesting than building thousands of replicas of grandma's dollhouse."

Noah handed Vic the book and he thumbed through the pages again. "Well, some of these features will be easier to build in a dollhouse than others. Japanese Hajitomi, which look like window shutters you can remove, would be tough, and people may lose them, but it's a nice idea. Guess I'll ask Wyoming next time I see him in my sleep."

They both chuckled.

"Why do you want to help me?" Vic asked. "Don't you want to finish your work with Soradin and get out of Quelter?"

"Sure, I'll keep working for them. Make a paycheck. But this sounds like fun."

Vic pulled out a pill container with "Made by Soradin" printed on the side. "It's for my cholesterol," he said. "I really don't take them like I should." Even Gale didn't know Vic wasn't taking his medication like he should. Noah, being a loner in town, was honored to know something about somebody.

When Vic got home, he cut the plastic off his grandmother's old dollhouse, which was perfectly intact. The white outside paint had dulled some, but everything else looked good as new. He marveled at the plainness of the kitchen, with its pink fridge, mini stove, mini table for dolls, and white wallpaper with tiny plastic blue flowers on it.

One of the kids' rooms was specially decorated by his grandmother. He knew this because she grew up to be a pilot, and the room had drawings of planes all over waxy orange paper. Vic felt connected to her through this little dollhouse, and wondered what type of connections dollhouses could create in a disconnected world.

# 5

# *Culture Entrepreneurs*

oradin, the world's biggest tech company, boasted its employee-centered approach, as illustrated in their employment ads:

"We stoke the fire of your ambition and put mentors in your life—people who will gently challenge you when you're down and frustrated. Our company knows that a strong mission and strong relationships lead to growth. At Soradin, you'll feel at home."

Soradin dominated the tech sector of the economy. By this point in time, the technology sector also managed the world's farming, transportation, energy, and entertainment. Another sector, "human services", encompassed teachers, waiters, and the few retail people left on the planet. The third, called "public service", encompassed law makers on a local level. This sector made small decisions on a day-to-day level. Larger governments were dismantled by Soradin in a campaign to convince the world to free itself of unjust governments and shift its loyalty to individual desires. There had also been something called the "Great Push," which successfully developed the poorer nations on Earth. This push created a global values system driven by consumption and entertainment, a world where people found little reason to wage war or protest or really be passionate about anything.

The company's CEO, Sonata Geraldine, wrote the ad herself. Sonata was introduced in public speeches as a "complex, yet serene piece of classical music." Her persona put people at ease, attracted the best talent in the world, and distracted the public as the company gobbled up businesses from all the major sectors of the global market.

She was tall and beautiful, but not in the conventional sense. At 43, her brown hair had become streaked with gray, which she didn't care to remove. Her fair skin was wrinkled under her eyes, with parallel and diagonal lines across them, like a river running down a hill on a topographic map. Her long nose changed its angle a quarter of the way down from her brow, making her conventionally ineligible for a lead role in a hit movie. But her essence was beautiful; friends claimed her spirit drifted and swirled around her body, like smoke from incense.

Her small apartment and modest possessions were a result of the simple living bandwagon other extremely wealthy people had begun to swear by. The places felt cozy with family pictures, knick-knacks, old books, and cultural artifacts. The apartment only had one computer, which lived in a work room, but to enter the room, Sonata had to send a text to an AI machine back at the office. In the text, she must explain the reason for entering the room, and if AI determines it urgent, she could enter. Sonata set it up that way to avoid computer time at home, time she could instead spend reading, knitting, cooking, seeing friends, running on the treadmill, or cherishing and cleaning up her keepsakes. Her life was a perfect combination of simplicity and abundance.

With her career being so central in her life, relationship opportunities passed Sonata by like interesting buildings from the window of a train. "One day I'll go see that old Greek Orthodox Church," one may say. Similarly, Sonata would meet a man, and in a few days he would call her, and inevitably go to voicemail. After hearing the voicemail, Sonata would think something like, "I should call him, I remember his sense of humor was really refreshing." Then weeks later, she'd wonder "wasn't I going to call that guy?" Intimate relationships for her, and for billions of people like her, had become a block to self-advancement and therefore not a priority.

A week after Wyoming's disappearance, Sonata met with Baelen, the team lead at the Culture Lab project in Quelter, to discuss how to handle the opening event publicly and check in on progress at Culture Lab. Before meeting him, she greeted three people in her building, as she did every day. First, she found Tim, working in his cubicle on the 14th floor of Sonata's headquarters.

"Hey Tim, do you have a minute?"

"For you I do," he replied. He closed his social media window, accepting that Sonata already noticed he was off task.

"Tim, if you could improve one thing about your life, what would it be?"

"I'd probably find a"—he wanted to say he'd find a new job, half jokingly, but steered clear of that idea—"find a dog that is really for me. The last dog our family had was good with the kids, but kind of boring and dense. I could take him camping, but doubt he'd even bark at a bear if came near the tent."

"I see. Tim, what's stopping you from doing that?"

"Oh, I probably just don't have the time for a dog."

There was an awkwardness to the conversation, stemming from Tim's awareness that Sonata was just checking off a box by talking with him.

"Well, Tim, thanks for sharing a little more about you. I have to run. Have a wonderful day."

Tim feigned a half smile. "You too, Sonata."

After she left, he flicked his baseball player bobblehead and said to himself, "Well, I am not sure that could have been more awkward." Yet he appreciated his awkward interaction with her, because it was better than no interaction at all. For years people were working from home, but Soradin was shelling out millions in health claims related to psychotherapy and meds for anxiety, depression, and other strange new mental health problems. More recently, they'd decided to bring people back to the office simply because it reduced their health-related costs.

Baelen and Sonata met in a smaller boardroom, with a five-by-eight cherry wood table, leather chairs, and a slim granite slab hanging from the wall with water running down it. On the other side of the room was a large flatscreen. The two sat closer together, one on each side of the right angle of the table.

"Can I get you something to drink?" Sonata asked.

Baelen loved when his boss waited on him. "Grapefruit seltzer water, please."

Sonata ordered the drink from her watch, and they got right into the project.

"Any news on Wyoming?" she asked.

"Nothing. I just don't get it."

"So he pointed out how we were just creating Culture Lab to sell stuff? I don't see it that way," Sonata said, optimistically and naively.

"Sonata, I know you see this project as a spark to the engine of creativity in this dull, monochromatic, apathetic world, but you know the board sees it otherwise. By unplugging people from the dominant culture, we'll be able to see their most fundamental desires, and from there create an amazing product line."

She pursed her lips and nodded in acceptance to his comment, but not in submissiveness to it. "Well, I hope Wyoming is okay."

They shared their moment of silence before moving on to business.

"How many participants do you have?" asked Sonata.

"We have 50 people. We got them within an hour of opening up the opportunity online. Great job to whoever crafted this ad, Sonata."

The online ad, posted on social media, read:

"Have you been feeling like this world is preventing you from who you are trying to become? Ever feel like society sucks out all the good ideas in you? Do you feel like you must become a brilliant inventor or else you're useless? Take part in this exciting three-year study on finding meaning and purpose in the modern world. You will join other courageous people by living outside of society's expectations for three years, and you will return with a sense of a child's wonder and curiosity. Take part in an exciting opportunity to unplug from your life. You will be compensated for your time."

"I wrote this," said Sonata, in a tone of self-aggrandizement, "but I wonder if it's a bit misleading. I am not telling them they will be seeds to entirely new cultures."

"That could put too much pressure on them," replied Baelen.

"Good point, so when will everything kick off?"

"March 20th, the first day of spring. We've been using a lot of blossoming language in our correspondence with the participants, and the garden in the compound is loaded with flowering plants*."

Sonata smiled. "Wonderful. Two weeks. I am excited. So, what is your biggest fear about opening?"

Baelen wanted to say something neutral, but sided with honesty. "Oh, that people will feel overwhelmed and want to leave after a few days."

Sonata sighed and replied, "That's bound to happen. That's okay. The important thing is to assure them they are taking part in something that can truly benefit humanity. Make sure they know this will be right up there with the impact of the counter-culture movement centuries ago."

Just then, Sonata got a call on her cell phone. Only twenty people had her number, so she asked Baelen to excuse herself and took the call.

---

*Plus that is the birthday of this novel's writer's brother. RIP Michael, love ya.

"Hey dad, what's up?"

"You wouldn't believe what happened to me last night," Vic said.

"Another nightmare?" she asked.

"Not exactly. But there was a dream. Some figure appeared to me in the clouds, someone who looked like that guy Wyoming who went missing. Sonata, I woke up with ten million in my bank account."

Sonata figured he was joking and went along with it. "Finally, you take some help from somebody! I don't know why you never accepted any money I tried to give you, dad."

"I'm being serious! This guy came to my dream, promised me ten million dollars, and now that's in my bank account. And I am supposed to build doll houses with it!"

"Okay, calm down dad. I have to finish a meeting. I'll fly to Quelter tonight and be at your house by dinner time."

Sonata walked back through the glass doors into the board room. "Baelen, I need to make plans to see my dad for dinner. I think he may be getting some kind of dementia."

"There is only one kind… but yeah, sure, no problem. I'll get all the final details in order. Have a safe trip."

Sonata smiled and left.

Baelen sat at his computer and opened up his "Culture Lab Grand Opening" spreadsheet. "I need a break," he said to himself.

He took a sip of his water and got into his phone. He opened an app where he could see his little science experiment in real-time. Since his position with Culture Lab began, he'd been growing bacteria in petri dishes as a hobby. To him, it was impossible, as one person, to see the spread of new cultural ideas in real-time throughout a population. But the spread of bacteria was something he could observe. e fiFrom his app, he could see the bacteria from a swab of his phone surface was really spreading, making yellow and white globs all over the petri dish. Then he put his phone down and looked at it with a bit of disgust.

**6**

# *Slaughterhouse Dollhouse*

Vic sat in his living room, waiting for Sonata and reading distractedly while Gale worked out in their garden. He sat in his brown recliner with cushion covers made with different shades of thick, intersecting, coarse threads. He looked around the space, through the dusty air, at all the family photos.

In one, he stood next to Sonata with his arm around her. She was only 19 and had already started a successful data analytics company. The photo showed the two standing in the grass out front of the first office building she worked at. Vic looked happy for his daughter, but at the time he was absorbed in his own career as a therapist and a psychology researcher.

*And all that for what?* he asked himself. *A few mediocre rewards in research? Was all the time with those people really worth all the money they gave me?*

He walked over to the picture on the mantle and laid it down. Then Vic's mind snapped into the present. *Maybe*

37

*Sonata could help with the dollhouses, maybe she could take on the project when I die,* he thought. He felt a little pain in his chest and rubbed it until it went away.

Just then, Sonata arrived. She turned the knob on the front door but it wouldn't work. "Stupid lock."

She went to the back and tripped over some water hose coils, then ran into the recycling bin, which slammed against the side of the house. After collecting herself, she wondered what she would say to explain why she'd been so absent for so many years.

Just then, Vic opened the backdoor, walked out to porch, and put his hands on the railing. "You okay?"

"Dad, I'm fine. But I wish you'd wind up that hose someday." She remembered tripping over that same hose as a kid.

Vic smiled. "Like I've told you, it's such a pain to unwind it. Come gimme a hug."

Sonata walked up the stairs and pretended there hadn't been any space created between them due to the time apart. She stayed so focused on her career, she hadn't allowed herself to miss him for a long time.

"Dinner is about ready, you two," Gale announced from the kitchen. "Sonata, I need your help setting the table." Sonata realized the way Gale talked sounded like a home movie from the 20th century.

"I'd love to help, Mom."

Gale had prepared lamb stew with cornbread—Sonata's favorite. Sonata tried to make this dinner every now and then, but always felt like the meal came up short. Maybe she couldn't recreate a sense of home with just a meal, anyway. She would also need the aging kitchen, with its heavy oak table, worn cabinets, stained blue linoleum floor, and large set of windows looking out in the garden. That kitchen saw her through big changes, and somehow told her she could relax into them.

As Sonata helped set the table for dinner, all the rare China came out into the open. Few people on the planet kept old China in their kitchens. Despite most of the world's population working in the tech sector, people still moved every few years, and China simply became too much to lug around.

Everyone sat down. Vic folded his hands, closed his eyes, and bowed his head. Gale folded her hands and bowed her head, but didn't close her eyes.

Sonata looked puzzled. "Are you guys really still praying before meals?" she asked. Years had passed since they ate a meal together.

Vic didn't acknowledge her. "Bless us, O Lord, for these, Thy gifts, which we are about to receive from Thy bounty. Through Christ, our Lord. Amen." After performing the Catholic cross on his head, chest and shoulders, Vic pulled his head up and looked at Gale.

Then Gale said her Buddhist prayer:

"Together we take this food;
the first taste is to cut off all evil;
the second is to practice all good;
the third is to save all beings;
May we attain the way of the Buddha."

She bowed toward her food and then brought her head up and smiled at Sonata, who returned an awkward look.

"So what are you going to do with the money, Dad?" she asked.

"What money? Gale asked.

Vic gulped. "We have ten million dollars as of yesterday morning, my dear."

"What the heck are you talking about?" asked Gale.

"Sweetie, I had a dream, and this being in my dream told me to start a dollhouse business. He told me I'd have ten million dollars deposited in my account to get it off the ground. I woke up, checked our account, and there it was."

"Have you been taking your medications on time?" asked Gale.

A long forgotten twinkle radiated from Vic's eyes. "I need an accountant, a lawyer, a developer, a researcher, materials, workers, and more importantly, someone who can design dollhouses."

"Dad, can retired therapists get psychiatric evaluations for free?" Sonata asked with a smile.

"Sweetie, I haven't felt this alive in a long time. Will you just go along with me?"

"Okay, Dad. Where are you thinking of building these dollhouses?"

"In the old Slessinger slaughterhouse just outside of town, on Thorp Highway."

"Dad, the old slaughter house? It's kinda creepy."

"It's perfect. I need the building this week. I can pay two million."

"Your ten million will go quick, Dad. I can give you another ten million."

"Fine."

While Sonata was a little annoyed at her Dad's brazen attitude, she saw a new side of him. He wanted to take risks and accept help along the way. Ignoring the questionable premise that someone from Vic's dream gave him ten million dollars, Sonata saw the dollhouse project as just the creative venture her dad needed.

Conversely, Gale saw the project as a huge distraction from the retirement plans she'd already made with Vic. None of their plans included anything about dollhouses.

After dinner they all sat on the computer to check the bank account. "There must be some mistake," Gale said. "You have to report this."

"Sweetie, we've played by the rules all my life. We raised a beautiful daughter, made this house a home, and helped many people in this community. It's time to go for it, whatever 'it' is."

Gale nodded and said, "I need to go lay down. Sonata, give me a hug. It's been too long since I've seen you. Don't make it so long next time."

Events throughout the following week cleared the way for Vic's vision. The factory would have two long tables with people assembling dollhouses on them. The plan was to first recreate Vic's grandmother's dollhouse. Then they would build dollhouses based on types of homes from around the world. Variety in housing styles rapidly diminished during the Earth's blanket period, but thankfully, Noah let Vic borrow Dalton's little red book as an essential reference.

When Vic was in his 30s, Soradin's servers crashed and trillions of websites were lost. Despite the collective belief that it could never happen, a solar storm caused the crash.

Along with vital information used to help people, so much trivial social media information disappeared in an instant, causing some people to call the event "The Useless Thought-Purge." Any paper reference to the past became immediately more valuable, but only to some. The prevailing view stated people couldn't advance if they looked back in time—a belief that locked the past in a tornado shelter, only to be entered during a severe weather event.

Twelve stations would fill the Slessinger Slaughterhouse, each building a different type of house people somewhere on the planet lived in. There was a hut from the Bushman people of the Kalahari, a mud house with metal roof from the slums of Rio De Janero, an actor's mansion in LA, a mud home in Mexico with a metal roof and clothes line outside; one of a cottage from rural Germany, one of a homeless person's rudimentary wood structure, originally built in Seattle, A Siheyuan home—typical in northern China—surrounding a court yard. There would be a conventional middle-class American house; one from a tenement housing apartment complex modeled after those in the Bronx. Then, a double-wide trailer and dollhouses that represented the living quarters of politicians within government buildings.

The team Sonata assembled took Vic and Noah's sketches and designed the unusual dollhouses without help from a computer program. They then sent the designs to a Soradin manufacturer to put the assembly kits together. In a manilla envelope with the designs, the manager wrote, "I know you are wondering why we would ever produce something like this, but this project is run by Sonata herself. Gotta do what the boss says."

Within a week, Vic bought the old slaughterhouse out on Slessinger Road. Discolored bricks and murky windows gave the building a traditional small operation slaughterhouse look. It had a chimney for gasses to escape and the many windows reminded employees to stay connected to living things. Tall, golden grass surrounded the building. In the front of the house, the grass went to the edge of the interstate highway and continued on to the rolling yellow hills beyond. Blackbirds sang in the fields, and sparrows built nests under the eaves. Beauty grew around the place and smothered death.

Vic and his new team began cleaning the facility on an early spring day, preparing it for a new use. Some of the old slaughterhouse equipment remained, including the chains to hang cattle upside down. They identified an area where they could assemble the dollhouses—a long room previously used for cutting finer pieces of meat—and put new tables across the room for people to assemble dollhouses alongside each other.

Throughout the day, Vic walked by a room in the slaughterhouse and got a strange feeling about it. The room had white tiles with gray, aging caulk covering all the walls, and Vic couldn't tell what the room was intended for. Eventually, he entered the strange space and could tell one of the walls had an area that looked blurry, so Vic walked over to the spot and reached into the semi-transparent material. While his hand was in the wall, his mind flooded with a vivid memory from his childhood:

Vic sat on an old brown couch next to his mother, playing with her long brown hair as she played solitaire. Her dry, shiny hair cooled him down on the hot summer day.

Just then, Vic felt her hair through the wall! A current ran through his body, and his mother's comfort gave him the feeling his whole life had gone according to plan, with nothing to make up for. He began crying, with his right hand still immersed in the wall.

"Vic?" Gale called from the other room.

"Um… I'll be right there," he said. He savored the experience until it disappeared, then pulled his hand out of the wall. Thinking the mysterious being from his dream re-entered the conscious realm, Vic asked out loud, "Wyoming, are you in here?"

No reply.

"Vic, I need your help," yelled Gale.

"Okay, I am coming, just a sec."

He walked into the other room, where Gale stood next to a box, waiting for him.

"I thought some décor in here would be nice, so I have some succulents and string lights and whatnot in this box, but I can't carry it any farther because my back is hurting."

"Sure thing," Vic replied. He grabbed the box, and they both went into the room with the long tables and set it down on one of them.

"Before you open this up, I want to show you something," he said in a pensive voice.

"Okay?" replied Gale in a concerned tone.

Vic grabbed her hand and led her into the room. They stood in the doorway, staring at the blurry wall.

"What's wrong with the wall?" Gale asked.

"Sweetie, I realize when the minister married us years ago, he never said 'through sickness and health, major cash gifts, and portals to other dimensions,' but I think there is some kind of memory portal over there."

"What?"

Vic led Gale to the wall.

"Stick your hand in," he said. "Just trust me."

"What?"

"Stick… your… hand… in."

She looked at him and knew by his eyes he wasn't lying. They both kneeled near the portal, and when she stuck her hand in, a memory flooded her mind:

She was eleven years old, having a picnic with her family at the park. Her hand ran through the green blades of grass. The clouds passed somewhat quickly in front of the sun, casting light and shadows on the grass field. Normally, Gale and her mother bickered at the park about what Gale wore or what friends she had, but this time her mother looked at her with gentle green eyes and said, "You make me so proud dear." Tears welled in Gale's eyes.

Just then, with her hand in the portal, Gale felt the grass. She closed her eyes and breathed deeply, then opened her other hand for Vic to hold.

"Good one, I see," said a man's voice from the other end of the room.

Gale pulled her hand out and looked at Wyoming, who stood in the doorway at the other end of the white tile room with his hands gripping the trim on the doorframe. Gale and Vic stood and walked to the side wall of the room, bracing themselves by putting their hands behind them on the wall.

"Is this the guy from the dream?" asked Gale with a trembling voice.

Vic looked at her and nodded.

Wyoming wore a white button-up shirt with khakis. He looked totally human, although Vic and Gale knew he wasn't. Vic knew he wasn't human because he transformed into some different form that night at the restaurant, while Gale suspected he wasn't human because her arm hairs stood up in his presence.

"What are you doing here?" Vic asked Wyoming. "And what the heck is this thing?"

Wyoming took his hands off the doorframe and walked a few steps into the room. "I came to see how your new mission was coming along. And that's a memory portal. One thing about culture—it requires powerful memories to keep being transmitted. If we never form emotionally vivid memories, we struggle to form strong values and traditions."

"Are you saying people are not forming 'emotionally vivid' memories, as you call them?" asked Vic.

"Well, yes. People now spend so much time alone on computers, I am afraid they are no longer forming lasting memories. Days blur into weeks and so on. Do you remember the virtual reality game where you could create characters with qualities of loved ones and then go on seemingly real adventures together?"

"Yeah, it wasn't too popular."

"Of course not, not nearly as stimulating as many of the other games. Vic, and Gale, when you are building these dollhouses I want you to imagine how they will create new memories in people. I want you to imagine them bringing people together."

"Yes sir." Vic gave a mocking salute.

"What about the portal?" asked Gale.

"What portal?" replied Wyoming.

The two looked at the portal wall, which now appeared normal. They walked over to it and felt the cold, solid tiles with their fingers. When they looked back at Wyoming, he was gone.

# 7

# *Welcome to Your New Life*

On the same day that Vic and Gale experienced their first memory portal in Quelter's Slaughterhouse, Culture Lab hosted its grand opening.

Sonata decided to host the project in a big blue house with white trim and a front porch with Adirondack chairs waiting to seat people. A wealthy family interested in the slower pace of Quelter tried living in the house years back but found the excitement and pace of the rest of the modern world too exhilarating to leave permanently. The house couldn't accommodate fifty volunteers, plus staff, so building developers at Soradin figured out how to create additional levels underground, to keep the country home vibe maintained.

Opening day of Culture Lab was not without hiccups. "The welcome banner is crooked. And where are our chefs?" Baelen yelled at his assistant. "Our first participants will be here in under an hour!"

The welcome banner hung on the house's front porch, baring "Welcome to your new life."

"Sorry, sir, I'll have the banner fixed. The chefs are on their way."

"Thanks. Anything you want to update me on?"

"Nope. Just know you are doing a great job, sir, and it's all going to be awesome."

"Save the positivity for three months from now when everyone begins to get bored of this place."

Baelen hadn't chosen this job, he was relocated here by Soradin, but he mustered all the enthusiasm he could for Sonata's grand idea to renew human culture. Maybe if this project took off he could go back to leading the shipping and receiving department.

Just then, the first two volunteers, Cecilia and Arush, walked through the open doorway.

"Welcome!" said Baelen, who insisted on greeting each volunteer personally. "You must be…"

"Arush." They shook hands, awkwardly.

"And Cecilia, right?"

"Yeah, do you have everyone's name memorized from our pictures?"

"No, just you two," said Baelen, making an attempt at a joke.

"Nice place. Looks like some ancient farm home I read about online," said Arush.

"Wait until you milk the cows."

This time he got a laugh from Cecilia, who really needed it. She'd spent the last decade as a professional writer who wrote about relationships, yet she struggled with her own. Despite her desire to find someone to start a family with, she was still looking at 35. Jadedness weighed her down like lead boots.

"You can both check in at the desk behind me," said Baelen. "They'll take all your electronic devices and show you to your rooms. Breakfast will start in half an hour."

A white plastic table with foldable legs was in the living room to the right of the entry-way. The large room had nice white tiles, amplified in brightness by the absence of furniture in the area. Arush and Cecilia approached the women at the table with a mix of enthusiasm and apprehension.

"Good morning. Can you give me your names, please?"

"Wow, I haven't heard a good morning in years," said Arush. "Love how traditional this place is. My name is Arush Kundali."

"I'm Cecilia. Could be under Ceci."

"Are you two together?"

They looked at each other and back at the woman.

"No," said Ceci. "We just happened to arrive at the same time."

"Well, you are both beautiful," said the woman.

In their mid-thirties, both Arush and Ceci were single. Arush stood at 6'2", had jet black hair, and dark brown eyes. He wore white or gray t-shirts and slim cut blue jeans practically every day. Ceci also had jet black hair, coming from her mother's Japanese side of the family. Both of them took great care of their bodies, yet they wondered when they would get noticed. In a world where everyone, all ten billion people, focused on their career until 40, a collective sense of inadequacy soaked in, solely due to all that time spent without romantic validation.

"Oh, I see you here Arush, and here you are Ceci. Here are your nametags. Please give me your devices."

They turned over their smart watches, smart glasses, smart phones, tablets, and laptops. They turned over the emotional security they thought these devices provided.

"Thank you," Ceci said. "By the way, looks like you need to get some furniture in here."

The women rolled her eyes and sighed. "Say what you want to say," she prompted.

"I just think…" Ceci paused. "Well, I am kinda uncomfortable with spaces that feel like a void."

"Much better," the woman replied. "You two are in rooms F and R, downstairs. The staircase is down the hall and to your left. Your room doors are open. Breakfast is in twenty minutes."

"Yes, sergeant," replied Arush.

"Try again," replied the woman.

"You're just really direct. I'm not used to it."

The woman smiled at the more sincere response. "Now go," she said.

The first two volunteers to arrive at Culture Lab walked down the hall, which lacked anything on the walls, and down the carpeted staircase to their rooms. Their bedrooms were furnished with a twin bed, nightstand, study desk with paper, and a cushion on the floor for meditation. Arush walked right into his and put his stuff on the bed, while Ceci stood in the doorway and sighed at the simplicity of her room.

Arush poked his head back out. "Just today," he told her. "You just have to get through this first day. I think it will get easier."

Ceci stepped in. They both cleaned up by taking cold showers to make sure they were fully awake for their first day.

In half an hour, they both came out of their of rooms. Arush looked at Ceci in the hall and said, "I think we're late. I have an impeccable sense of time, but somehow I sense it cracking by just being here."

"I think it's okay," Ceci replied. "I think we can be late for stuff here."

After walking up to the main level, they looked through the dining area and out the glass sliding doors to notice people gathering for breakfast out back. The back patio was massive, with ten round tables meant for five people each. A canvas tent covered most of the area to keep the group dry in case of a spring rain.

They sat down with some other participants and struck up awkward conversation until being invited to the breakfast tables to serve themselves. People were excited but suspended their faith.

"Do you think this is all going to work?" Ceci asked.

"What do you mean by work?" Arush asked.

Ceci put her lips together and moved her mouth to the side, just a little, while she thought of what to say. "I mean, are we going to really change, like at our core? And even if we do, how long will it be before the ravenous world changes us back? I just keep thinking of this gate my dad taught me to fix. It was really sagging, so we attached this cable from one corner to the other and tightened it to keep the gate upright, but in two months it was sagging again."

"Why didn't your dad just buy a new gate?" asked a man sitting at their table.

"That's not the point," Ceci replied.

"Forgive me," said the man. "I am just bored and want to be part of the conversation."

Arush looked at Ceci with understanding in his eyes. "I get what you are saying. Many of the people here pride themselves as 'thought-leaders.' They've run workshops on being extraordinary. They talked to full auditoriums, with millions of plays online. Their ideas on how to be in family, how to love, how to forgive, made them creators of new cultural values. But these values couldn't stick, not in a world that gobbles up powerful speeches just like dog trick videos. So we are all here, desperately hoping Culture Lab offers something different.

Ceci smiled at feeling understood, and her dark brown eyes had just a bit of twinkle. "If it does nothing else, it could give people a long break from their phones," she said.

"Hmm. Excuse me, everyone," Baelen said. "I'd like to give our opening speech now."

Ceci and Arush finished their bites and turned toward the stage where Baelen stood. All the participants were sitting in white round tables on a big grassy back yard with nice fencing around it. Lights strung from trees across the lawn draped from above. Lights also lined the framing around the stage where Baelen stood with his podium and mic stand.

He'd worked with a speechwriter to make the opening speech as grandiose as possible. "We are so happy you are here. Culture Lab offers a reboot—a reboot that will ripple throughout the world. As the leading technology company globally, Soradin recognizes our failed attempts in the past to educate people about the limits of technology. We have installed applications to show people their usage, and have even started campaigns for wise social media use in schools, but the data coming back to us showed that people were still isolating more and more, and we saw the dreams they created as kids getting replaced with fantasies of who they wanted to be online.

"Culture Lab is intended to remedy such social problems. Sonata, our CEO, was sitting in her humble apartment one night when she thought of it. She held up a picture of her, as a kid, with her grandmother. In the picture, Sonata held a ladybug while looking up at her grandmother with wonder. She began tearing up just staring at that picture and the experience was so visceral—all the senses came back to her and she dropped into them like a tank of cool water. Then she thought, *What if I could give these feelings the other people? What if they could have powerful memories again? Is it this one global culture narrowly focused on security and entertainment? Or the lack of true community?* She thought on this all night, and had a plan for Culture Lab in the morning.

"My guests, you've made a commitment to be here for three years. Of course, you are free to go anytime you want, but we suggest sticking through the first week before making a decision. In this first week you are going to experience various environments and narratives of others' experiences in them. You are going to act in plays as heroes and villains and anything in-between. You are going to eat meals slowly and you are going to sleep deeply."

People clapped, somewhat awkwardly. Slowing down didn't seem like something anyone should clap for. Baelen, reading the audience poorly, went on with the optional part of his speech. "My friends, we are living in what sociologists called 'the age of hyperactivity,' also known as 'the information age on speed.' You may have signed up for Culture Lab because you feel used by the tools you're supposed to be *using*, and you've come to see your self-help videos and monumental insights in social science are a trap. People are looking for entire cultures to give them purpose and continuity between the past and future. You began to see you couldn't offer that. You came to see the only way out was a total break from society."

Everyone clapped, still awkwardly.

"I'll take some questions now."

"What if this doesn't work?" asked Arush.

"Then you'll go back to inspiring people for brief periods in-between their greater swells of apathy, which isn't so bad, right?"

Arush smiled and felt a bit more trusting of Baelen.

"Next question," Baelen prompted.

Someone else asked a question on everyone's mind. "Okay, say I stick with this for three years, then what?"

"May I remind you to all read your commitment letters," replied Baelen, in a way that didn't point out the person asking the question for failing to read what he was supposed to. He went on to answer the question directly. "As your contract states, at the end of three years, you will each get $50,000 dollars in your account, in addition to whatever you had before arrival. $50,000 isn't much, but it will be enough to live off for six months, in the event you somehow lost everything you owned while living here."

"What if we like it so much at the end of the three years that we don't want to leave?" asked Ceci.

Baelen hadn't anticipated that question. "Then you can probably stay. I'm sure we can justify the cost in Soradin's budget." The audience smiled, and Baelen decided to end on a high note. But once they saw their bedrooms after dinner, none of the participants dreamed of staying past three years.

# 8

# *Play is a Noble Cause*

After spending a few days preparing the old slaughterhouse for dollhouse production, Vic and Gale went on a weekend retreat at a bed and breakfast out in Sandbush Hills, about an hour from town. Vic figured spending a little bit of Wyoming's windfall on the trip would reinvigorate him. Gale figured she would get some quality time with her husband before taking her own photography trip out to Sandbush.

Gale drove while Vic read about dollhouses in a book he'd found at the library. "Did you know a Chinese Dollhouse comes with a little pond, coy fish, and an arched footbridge? The houses even have ornate trim and warm yellow lighting made by tiny bulbs."

"And people are supposed to like this more than entering a virtual realm where they can build worlds, play sports, and pretend they are at war?"

"I wish you'd give me an ounce of emotional support with this," said Vic.

"Okay, I'll just tell you all your ideas are great," replied Gale.

Vic looked at her, but her eyes stayed on the road. "You are pushing it," he said. He put his hand on his chest and began to struggle to get big in-breaths. "Ahh. Ooohh," he moaned.

"Vic. What's going on?" Gale asked with a tone of denial, suspecting immediately that Vic was having a heart attack. Her father had one when she was a kid and showed all the same signs.

Vic didn't respond.

"Okay, I am taking you to the hospital."

"Ah. I'll be fine, just… need… some fresh air."

Then Vic went unconscious, and thoughts raced through Gale's mind. *He isn't supposed to die yet. We were supposed to get a cabin out in the Sandbush and completely fill up the front porch with… dollhouses. No NOT dollhouses… purple and green flower pots. We were supposed to see Sonata get married, even though it's getting late for that. We were supposed to… I can't be alone.*

The space after "I can't be alone" felt like being trapped deep in a cave with water rushing in.

Gale took a breath. She looked at Vic. He was still unconscious. She wanted to give him CPR but she really wasn't confident she could do that. She wanted to call 911 but didn't have service. It was very likely if Vic were alive, he wouldn't be for much longer.

Then Gale saw a big blue house on the side of the road with four vans out front. She figured he'd be dead by the time she tried to get him to the hospital, so why not take him here and see if they had a defibrillator? She took a left at the sign that said "Property of Soradin," drove down the dirt road, and prayed while dust swirled around her car.

After parking, she ran to the front door. "Group is out of the building," the sign said. Culture Lab was on day two and the participants were on their first excursion. She knocked louder. She was about to throw a rock through the window when Baelen came to the door.

"Hi, can I help you?"

"My husband has had a heart attack. Do you have a defibrillator?"

"Yes, we do. Where is your husband?"

"He is in the car."

"Okay, I'll be right back. Oh, and you can call 911 even if you don't get service. They are on a different signal entirely."

Baelen ran to the first aid closet and grabbed the device. By the time he got out to their car, Gale had finished her 911 call and laid Vic on the ground, in case chest compressions would be needed.

Baelen came out jogging, his skinny figure cutting through the spring breeze. "Thanks for putting him on the ground." He stuck one patch above Vic's left peck, and the other on his ribs below his right peck. "Okay, after giving him a shock, I'll give him chest compressions while the device charges."

Gale nodded.

She watched Baelen give a shock and then compressions for two minutes before the machine could re-analyze Vic's heart. She watched like she was in a training class, and her husband of 40 years was a dummy they were using to practice. A mixture of curiosity and shock stirred in her like oil and water.

After a two sets of compressions and shocks, Vic opened his eyes and took a breath. Baelen pulled his hands away quickly, as if just touching Vic could compromise his chances of recovery. Gale resisted the temptation to smother Vic as well.

Before noticing Baelen and Gale, Vic saw Wyoming smiling above him. He looked hand-drawn with pencil, on the white fluffy clouds. "You are on the right track," he said. "Your body is telling you no, but your soul is telling you yes. Keep listening to your soul."

Vic came to. "My ribs!" he winced in excruciating pain from the three ribs Baelen broke during compressions.

"Just lay still," Baelen directed Vic before shifting to address Gale. "Can you wait here while I grab him a pillow?"

"Where would I go?" she said, with a bit of an attitude.

Baelen went inside to the common area, grabbed a pillow off the blue couch in front of the fireplace, and glanced at the magazine on the coffee table. "Imagine your breath could fill a valley," read the cover. Outside, the white, sparkling gravel released most of its heat within a two-foot layer above the ground. Vic stared up into the sky, wondering if Wyoming would come back. Gale sat in the gravel beside him, wondering how she'd relate with him in the remaining time they had together.

Baelen came out with two water bottles. "Here," he said to Gale. "You must be thirsty and I am sure he is too, but I don't know if water is okay right after a heart-attack."

"The science is always changing, but I think water is always okay," replied Gale. She propped Vic's head up with her hand and gave him some sips from her water bottle.

"This is Vic, by the way, and I am Gale," she said to Baelen.

Baelen kneeled next to Vic to block the sun. He shook both their hands. "I'm Baelen, pleased to meet you. An ambulance is on the way.

"Thanks," said Vic. "So tell me, what is this secret operation you've got going out here? Are you doing some kind of psychological experiments with people?"

Baelen smiled. "You could say that."

Just then the image of a glass cube flickered in the light blue sky, and only Vic saw it. "What was that?" he said.

Baelen and Gale looked up and only saw blue sky.

"Nothing dear," said Gale.

Vic rubbed his eyes. "A glass cube. I just saw one. In the sky. What could that mean? Wyoming?"

"Just take it easy," said Baelen. "Let me get you a pillow to rest on."

As he came back outside with a pillow, Quelter's paramedics pulled into the driveway.

At the hospital, Vic's doctor recommended heart surgery, because his blockages were too severe for a stent. Vic was not interested in surgery at first, not interested in the idea of having his chest opened, but he had to weigh his fear of strangers opening his body—professionals, but strangers none-the-less—against his fear of death. He agreed to the surgery and scheduled it for the following week, but wasn't sure how he'd tell Gale. He always thought Gale perceived his stubbornness as a winning quality, even when she didn't agree with what he was being stubborn about. But this time she'd be happy he conceded.

On the way home from the hospital, Gale offered some comic relief to it all: "I told you not to order the Grand Slam the other night."

They both started laughing.

"Yeah, those damn Grand Slams. They should call them Grand Blockages," Vic said.

Gale's lips formed a half smile while her eyes expressed sorrow. "How do you want to spend the last years of your life? Making dollhouses? How about letting that go and moving to Sandbush with me like we planned?"

"Gale, sweetie, this is the most ridiculous, far-fetched calling anyone could embark upon. But Wyoming says the dollhouses will have far-reaching implications. You kinda got to believe a guy who can show up in your dreams, in the sky, and around memory portals.

"Maybe Wyoming brought us this project just to get the family closer," replied Gale in a hesitant tone. "I mean, Sonata is already spending more time with you than she has in years."

"Sweetie, humans have more gadgets and entertainment than ever. They can project recorded holograms of deceased loved ones from their phones. They can watch episodes from their favorite shows in their dreams. And yet the world is a drab place full of lost people looking for the meaning and connection culture used to bring them. Now culture just brings them more stuff."

Gale nodded throughout Vic's lecture, and then hesitated to say what she was thinking, but came out with it anyway. "These dollhouses are just *stuff*."

Vic didn't back down. "Yeah, I guess you're right. But these are something simple and pure. Something family can gather around and play with and tell stories with. People stopped telling stories because no one seemed to have the attention span for them. I think these dollhouses can change that."

"Hmmm…" Gale went inward, into an analysis of it all, as she drove down the open highway to Quelter. *Maybe he is right. Maybe this is a good idea. It just sounds ridiculous. Maybe he's trying to make up for the mediocrity of his career. Who cares? Maybe this is more about me wanting to go to Sandbush. Maybe I'll just take a trip there once Vic gets better. The rattlesnakes out on the rocks, capturing the heat from the warm spring days, would make for some great photos.*

"Why don't you just take a trip there?" asked Vic. "Instead of moving there?"

Sometimes Vic thought he read Gale's mind correctly, but was way off. Maybe his interactions with Wyoming had improved his telepathy.

"Okay, but we'd need someone here to look after you," replied Gale.

When they got home, Gale arranged for Noah to come over, and because he had nothing else going on, Noah came early, before Gale left.

When Noah arrived, he brought the little red book he got from Barbara Hunsaker. He thought he could sit and read it to Vic while he recovered. Instead, he sat with Vic and Gale, who postponed her trip after hearing about the book. For some time, the three talked about the various cultures highlighted by the book. They spent much of their time learning about Oracles among the Azande people in Africa. An Oracle, or Shaman, would reach into the jar of the spirit world, and pull out the causes of or solutions to certain unfortunate events, such as sudden illness or a drought. To access the spirit world, the Shaman had to poison a chicken. The chicken's fate provided insight into the issue. For example, if the chicken died, the drought would go on longer, but if it lived, the tribe could expect rain soon.

Noah thought it was ridiculous to trust the Oracle. "You could just as easily spin a wheel and make up whatever you want."

Vic saw it differently. "Putting a living creature's life at stake makes people take the Shaman seriously."

"That poor chicken," said Gale. "And people pay him to do this?"

Vic went on. "People spend billions of dollars in our culture for others to tell them why things happen a certain way. Spiritual healers, speakers, counselors, the list goes on and on. And much of it is just someone's opinion."

Gale rolled her eyes. "At least they don't kill chickens," she said.

They all laughed.

Noah looked back at the book. "Looks like the Oracle can also predict future disasters. In some cases the death of the chicken says a typhoon is coming, so people can prepare. Maybe the typhoon doesn't come when they say it will, but at least they'll be prepared for one when it does arrive."

After discussing the little red book for some time, they came to see how the seemingly impractical traditions and beliefs in these extinct cultures served to unify people against the vicissitudes of nature. Science leaped over many of nature's threats, but it lacked the cultural symbols and traditions to unify people. Indeed, Soradin had begun to control some weather problems, but a massive volcanic eruption or solar storm still posed a risk to humanity. The loss of culture created a greater issue—not knowing how to unite against shared problems.

Gale decided to stay home with Vic and at midnight, Noah left. He did not just leave Vic and Gale's home, but Quelter entirely. "I think I am going get out of this town," he'd said. "There has got to be a culture out there that's different than this."

"Where you going to go? And what about your job?" asked Gale.

"I'm going on an adventure. Going to look for people creating something different in their lives. I'll find a different job."

Vic looked disappointed. "Okay, suit yourself," he said.

Noah smiled and then went to the front door to leave. "The front door doesn't work right now, try the back door," said Gale in an embarrassed tone.

Noah turned around. "Kinda ruins my epic goodbye," he said, half jokingly.

As Noah walked around the side of the house, Vic had a sense that even though he was losing his friend, he'd soon gain another one. Experience told him that on previous missions in life, he met people who stayed in his heart forever. He knew there would be more to his current mission than building dollhouses.

# 9

# *Changing Culture with a Journal*

Inspiring speeches, great food, and undistracted social interaction filled the first few days at Culture Lab. Enthusiasm for the program shined out like a lighthouse on a dark sea.

Just as participants started getting comfortable, things changed. For the first few days, they could sleep until 7:30. On the fourth day, music jolted participants out of their sleep at 6 a.m.

As soon as he opened his eyes, Arush sat up. "What is this? I've never heard anything like it." He rubbed his eyes and combed back his black hair with his hand.

He looked at the small black speaker mounted in the corner of his room.

"If you wanna be my lover, you gotta get with my friends. Make it last forever, friendship never ends."

"Sounds like something from the 90s, he said to himself**.

------

**Spice Girls. "Wannabe". Spice. Matt Rowe, Richard Stannard. Virgin Records, 1996.

Is that the Spice Girls from the 1990s? Are they really making us wake up to *this?*

He hopped in the shower and then put on the usual black t-shirt, jeans, and lucky bracelet. By the time he stepped into the hallway outside his room, the sound from the intercoms placed throughout the building had changed.

"Each day, as part of your transformative experience here at Culture Lab, you will get jolted awake with earworms from the 1990s. The goal is to get songs stuck in your head to point of wanting either a lobotomy or a genuine desire to replace such music with something better. Feel free to visit our instrument library on the $2^{nd}$ floor, way down there, after breakfast." Baelen let go of the intercom button and basked in his power to give these morning announcements.

*Forgot my watch*, Arush thought. Culture Lab gave everyone basic watches, as they no longer had phones to track time.

He went back into his room, grabbed the watch from the wooden bedside table, put it on, and noticed he needed to make his bed. Like everyone else, Arush got a twin bed with blue sheets and a black comforter. Not a lavish comforter, nor an itchy gray army blanket. The Culture Lab team designed rooms to be comfortable, but not lavish, in order to encourage people to leave their rooms and be social.

He made the bed, then left the room.

*Where is breakfast?* he asked himself. *It's either on the patio out back or in the dining room. I hope they don't get mad because I am late.*

He looked at his watch. "6:30? How could it only be 6:30?" Breakfast wasn't until 6:45. Back home, it would take him at least 45 minutes until he was in the kitchen making breakfast. He didn't know exactly why it took longer to get ready back home.

As a software developer for Soradin, Arush rarely had meetings, so he never needed to develop the habit of being on time. But this started to change when he left Soradin and started his own catering business. Success in that career required punctuality, which Arush hadn't yet mastered.

He continued his search for breakfast, checking the patio first. Nearly everyone was already seated there, with a coffee, tea, or orange juice.

He found Cecilia's table right away. "Anyone sitting here?" he asked.

"All yours," she said. She scooted out the white foldable chair from the white round table.

"Wow, everyone is so punctual," he commented.

"We were just talking about that," said Cecilia. "Everyone at this table is habitually late.

Baelen went up to the podium. "Good morning everyone. Hope you slept well and woke with the same eagerness you possessed yesterday."

"Can I get some of your eagerness?" whispered Arush to Cecilia, trying to be cute.

"I only give out eagerness to those desperate for it," quipped Cecilia.

Baelen noticed Arush and Cecilia's conversation, but continued on. "Oatmeal and fruit will be served shortly. While we wait, I want to go over the day with you. Today we are going to a park on the outskirts of Naundine, a city ninety miles away that most of you are aware of. Because it's over the mountains, the environment there is different. It's technically a temperate rainforest. We are going to walk down into a ravine there and journal."

"Profound," said Arush. "So glad I gave up my life to journal in a cold and wet ravine."

"Will we have to sit on the ground?" asked Cecilia.

"I'm afraid so," replied Baelen with the grim tone.

"In all seriousness," said Baelen, "we spend so much time on devices, trying to manage various virtual identities, that we've forgotten how to be in touch with ourselves and reality. The present moment is a meadow with spring wildflowers yearning to be seen, and yet we're stuck wondering about our social media page, about typed responses to something we typed a few days back."

Cecilia wasn't satisfied. "Okay, but what does being in touch with myself have to do with spawning new cultures?"

Baelen gave a half smile and Cecilia couldn't see if his confidence was true.

"Great question," he said. "Being grounded in yourself frees you up to create without fear of criticism."

Cecelia gave him an incredulous look. She'd learned to be pushy through years of interviewing and writing. While she wrote on various psychological topics, she earned the most recognition for her work on opening up while questioning the intentions of the ego. At some point in her writing career, Cecilia saw people's pre-occupation with "enlightened relationships" ironically getting in the way of greater intimacy with the world. So she quit writing for a while. During her hiatus, she stepped into a snare by getting online and watching the popular speeches she gave. She saw all the talks she gave as ironically distant and impersonal. It was always easier for an expert to tell you what to do when they were 1,000 miles away from your life, she realized. In midst of her resignation from fame, she received a letter from Soradin inviting her to Culture Lab.

After breakfast, everyone got ready for their trip. They headed out in three large vans to the ravine in a city park known as "Volunteer Park." On the way to the ravine, one of the members joked, "We are volunteers in one really pointless experiment."

As volunteers traversed down the side of the ravine, off the trail, Arush asked Baelen, "Are you sure the city is allowing this?"

"No, I am not," replied Baelen, "but Soradin can pay the fine if we are found trespassing."

Arush felt the fear of breaking rules in his gut, but not for long. Once they got down the wet, fern-covered slope, they found an area near a trickle of a stream, with river rocks and downed logs to sit down. Baelen opened his backpack and pulled out a little red book.

"This guy, Noah, who used to work for Culture Lab, gave me this," he said. "In it are hundreds of journal entries written by a couple who loved to travel. The couple has long since passed, but they managed to make record of now extinct cultures. They also documented natural environments like this ravine, in fear of their ruin. Take a listen to this entry:

'... wet ferns covered everything, and water dripped down from the big leaf maple leaves above. The air right here in this ravine feels a bit cleaner than the air in the park...'"

After Baelen read the entry, participants pulled out their journals and jotted down their observations and interpretations. They began to reconstruct the concept of self as related to something else, in this case, the ravine. One participant even sketched a picture of himself walking out of the ravine into a void of space.

When they finished, they ate lunch, and after lunch they sat and listened to the sounds in the forest.

# 10

## *Time with People instead of Machines*

Tommy was a cute kid, seemingly innocent. But he portrayed innocence to be liked and trusted by adults who could give him attention. When he was eight, both of his parents went missing. They were at a tropical resort and they went to the beach at night. The following morning, all that was left on the beach was their towel and two empty wine glasses. Following the mysterious event, Tommy's aunt, Claire, adopted him and raised him for two years before noticing Tommy didn't fit the mold in school. She tried therapy with him, but the therapist said he demonstrated the emotional regulation of a fifteen-year-old. That's why he didn't fit in. He was too mature.

Tommy told his aunt he wanted to travel and go on adventures, and she wondered if such aspirations could help him fit in better than traditional school. So one day she called her old college friend Sonata. Well, she called Sonata's receptionist.

"Hi, I would like to speak with Sonata Geraldine. It's Claire Romanke, an old friend from college."

"She is in a meeting right now, but I can tell you she called," replied the receptionist.

To Claire's surprise, Sonata did actually call her back later that afternoon.

"Claire, it's been forever, how are you?"

"Good. Can't complain. I am a third grade teacher now. After college, I decided business wasn't for me."

"Fantastic, sounds nice. Much more mellow than what I've got going."

"Yes, I don't envy your job, Sonata, but the money would be nice."

"I wish I had a family," said Sonata candidly.

"Well, maybe I could help with that," replied Claire.

"What do you mean?"

"I adopted my sister's child, Tommy. His parents unfortunately went missing on a tropical vacation. He's really a sweet kid, but also an adventure seeker. I was wondering if Soradin offered any summer adventure programs for kids? Maybe you could be his mentor or something."

"Sorry to hear about your sister, Claire. Yes, we do programs, but I may be able to offer something else for the kiddo."

"Okay, say more."

"I am running a project called Culture Lab. We are taking fifty highly influential adults out of their normal routines and putting them together with the hope of growing new human cultures."

"I always admired that about you, Sonata. You just get an idea and go with it."

"Thanks. You gotta learn to accept big failures living that way, though."

"So why would this Culture Lab appeal to an eleven-year-old?"

"Well, I remember being in this mentoring program for girls, and I worked with a kid who was ten or eleven, I can't recall, who lost her parents. She showed remarkable maturity for her age, along with an openness to travel. I think the loss opened the doors to life stages that other people just have to wait to discover."

"Interesting. What kind of adventures does Culture Lab go on?"

"The group explored an old ravine yesterday. They found some artifacts and wrote in journals. Like pen and paper journals, because they don't have phones to take notes in. Next week they are going to a museum of the past with projections of the future. They'll go to other countries, but we both know the cultures there are no longer any different than here."

"Sounds fun. Are the people safe?"

"Oh yeah, all participants are vetted by our people at Soradin. Also, I'll work with the program manager, Baelen, to make sure Tommy is safe.

"Okay, I'll tell Tommy about it and see what he thinks."

"Bye Claire Bear."

"Bye Moonlight Sonata."

Many people at Soradin wondered why Sonata didn't make Culture Lab a camp for kids. Wouldn't it make more sense to grow new cultures with young people? Sonata realized this whole experiment could create psychological problems when they reintegrated with modern society. The point was to spread their newly acquired cultures, but if they couldn't, adjusting to the new world culture could be traumatizing for kids. But Sonata had a hunch that for Tommy, it would be an adventure.

Back at Culture Lab, people were getting into the swing of things. They kept writing and performing plays and planning out places they wanted to go with the budget provided by Soradin. Over the week leading up to the museum trip, they developed a great sense of comradery. Before Culture Lab, comradery was just a word in the dictionary. It was rarely felt, because people worked in such isolation from each other, and interactions were mostly through computers.

On the day of the seemingly boring museum trip, Baelen gave a little speech to prepare everyone:

"Today we are going to the Skip Through Time Museum. I want you to know the guides on our tour will talk to you like ten-year-olds. This is not meant to demean or manipulate you, it is meant to bring up old memories which have fallen deep into your mind under the weight of constant information and social pressure."

"As long as we get candy," Cecelia said.

"You'll have to pay museum gift shop prices," replied Baelen, clearly missing the joke.

"Then I am out," Cecelia said, feeling more comfortable to be herself in this group.

## 11

# *Dollhouses for a World of Condos*

Normally, the group would have visited the museum gift shop after their tour, but they had a long drive and some of them forgot to pack snacks. As Ceci waited in line to buy an overpriced candy bar, an eleven-year-old boy tapped her on the side.

"Can you get me a Saw-Wickers?" he asked.

Ceci looked at him curiously. "Where is your mom?"

"Missing," the boy replied.

Her curious face, lifted with enthusiasm, dropped. "Excuse me?"

Baelen stepped in. "This is Tommy," he said. "I meant to introduce him formally, but this was the only time his mom—"

"Guardian," Tommy interrupted.

"Yes, thank you for correcting me. The only time his guardian was able take off work to drop him off with us."

Tommy looked at Baelen. "Could *you* buy me a Saw Wickers?" he asked.

"Sure," said Baelen.

Saw Wickers chocolate bars were named after a man who pioneered resistance movements in recent history, such as the Down with Tech Life Movement. This movement fought for the creation of a civilization with one fundamental tenant: fifty percent of the time in ones' waking life had to be spent with other people. It fought the cycle of draining hours on machines to make others' jobs and lives more efficient. Hours given to others so they could, in turn, spend more hours on machines. The movement created a few small pilot communities, but Saw Wickers called it quits when Soradin offered him two billion to step down as leader of the movement. Now his life is a "food for thought" bio printed on the back of a chocolate bar.

"Before we go in," said Baelen, "I want you all to meet Tommy. Tommy is the son of a friend of Sonata's. He is fascinated about our journey here, and he's here to remind us to have fun."

"That's right," replied Tommy, as he folded tin foil back, approaching his last bite of chocolate.

As the group finished their snacks outside the giftshop, a museum guide walked over. "Okay, is your group ready?"

"Yep," replied Baelen.

The guide looked at Tommy. "Please throw away the wrapper before coming in."

"Oh dang, I was to planning shape it into something that looks old, like the other stuff here, and then make you think I stole something," Tommy replied.

"Very funny," said Baelen.

The guide looked at the group. "Is this everyone," he asked?

"Well, this is 25," said Baelen. "We split our group in two, and you'll see the next group in an hour."

"Gotcha. Okay everyone, the theme of the museum this month is living off the land. As of around forty years ago, the last group of people known to grow, forage, or hunt food for themselves integrated into our culture, the one world culture known as the Great Unity."

"What about in towns like Quelter," asked Arush. "Don't the people there have gardens?"

"Yes," replied the guide. "But they are so small. We are really only referring to people who got 10% or more of their diet through gardening, foraging, or hunting."

Arush nodded, and the guide went on. "We will first see an exhibit on the Kalahari Bushman in Africa, who forage for nuts and berries in a semi-desert. Then we will look at communes in Hawaii, and then farmers in Eastern Europe."

By the time they reached the Hawaii Communes exhibit, Arush began wondering if Tommy joined them for some other hidden reason.

"I can't really explain why, but I don't like the kid being here," he told Cecilia. "What if he is some sort of spy?"

Cecilia found Arush's concern amusing. "You think this kid is a spy? What sort of secret information will he get? Do you think our museum scavenger hunt cards hold the key to something incredible?"

The most visceral of all the exhibits was the post-apocalyptic one. There were two miniature representations under the glass display case surrounded by curious, pensive viewers. The left scene depicted a revolution. Garbage cans were filled with smartphones and billboards were in flames.

"Who am I?" was graffitied all over the little brick walls and toy cars in the scene. The presenter at the museum told the group the side of the scene showed a society where no one belonged. As a result of all the confusion, people revolted. The right side of the scene depicted what happened after the revolt: Amish-looking farmers on a utopian-looking pasture.

"In this scene, 'who am I' is spray painted on the barn…"

"Didn't that question get worked out for people after the revolution?" asked Ceci.

"Not exactly," replied the guide. "According to the designer of this exhibit, the adults lived in total bliss, yet in ignorance. They created a world with culture based on *not* being something else. They failed to recognize culture responds to the environment, builds on itself, and requires tremendous amounts of creativity. Teenagers in the group painted those words. The new utopian world created for them lacked options for their self-expression."

"I'm bored, when is this presentation over?" asked Tommy.

Everyone in the group laughed. It was good to have a kid on board.

The dollhouse factory launched production just a few days after Vic's recovery from his heart attack. A few workers from Soradin with diverse backgrounds helped design the various types of dollhouses, which represented a time before cultural sameness cast a shadow over the planet. Now Quelter community members were helping Vic and the Geraldine family assemble the first five hundred dollhouses in this small factory, to test the difficulty of assembling them, and to come together in community.

When the Slessinger Slaughterhouse was active, workers parked in front and entered in through the side, where they filled out their timecard before going to work. Now, a sign in the parking lot told dollhouse workers to enter through the front through the office. Gray corrugated metal covered all four sides of the building and the roof. When it was operational, trucks loaded with cattle came around the back and let the cows out into a muddy field. Alongside the field ran a creek with oak and alder trees on the bank. With Slessinger closed for years, the creek now ran clean.

The parking lot was 600 feet from the main road. If you turned your back to the slaughterhouse from the parking lot, you'd see a dirt road running to the main road, a few signs, endless golden bunchgrass, a few juniper trees, and a few homes off in the distance.

After just a few days in operation, Vic started showing up much earlier than everyone else. Each morning, he made coffee with the coffee maker he placed in his office and sat in the weathered desk chair left as an homage to the manager who'd spent forty years at Slessinger. He looked at the wall with small tears in the shiny brown wallpaper that rolled back to expose the cheap wood beneath. "Maybe in a parallel universe I'd manage a slaughterhouse instead of doing therapy," he said to himself.

After a week in operation, Sonata paid a visit. She entered the building with a purple windbreaker, as spring days in Quelter seemed to step toward summer and other times away from it.

"I wasn't expecting you," Vic told his daughter.

"Well, Mom told me you are having open heart surgery in two days."

"Yeah, yeah. Two days before they saw me open. I mean, laser me open. Hey, I put together our first dollhouse last night. Wanna see it?"

"Wow, Dad, you seem pretty calm for a someone who's about to have a major operation."

"I realized I have no other choice. This dollhouse is spectacular. Come see it."

They went through the room with all the freezers and into the main workroom. There, at the end of two long tables, stood Vic's dollhouse right next to his grandmother's.

Only the color of the outside walls of the two dollhouses differed. Vic's grandma's was painted blue, while Vic's was red. In both dollhouses, a brick chimney climbed up from the bottom level to the top. The rooms were full of relics from the 20th century: mini toy cars, antique chests, posters, sports trophies, a framed fish, a little red wagon, and miniature dolls. In the middle level bedrooms of the three storied dollhouses, small plastic kid figurines laid on their stomachs and played a board game. Brown wall paper lined the bedrooms and the living room downstairs. All the brown made the white kitchen, with its blue countertops, gleam.

A fire, painted on the glass of the fireplace in the living room, provided warmth to the imagination. Above the mantle, a mini-pendulum clock ticked away and chimed on the hour. The house stayed true to the past, and seeing the past in front of him gave Vic the visceral feeling his life was a continuum of past and future. Recognizing his position in the unfolding of the collective human experience gave Vic a sense of self-acceptance and purpose. He had found a connection out of reach for the 22$^{nd}$ century, self-actualized techno-human, responsible for developing an entirely distinct culture within himself.

Vic noticed tear of joy running down Sonata's cheek and said, "Don't you just love the look of natural cedar?"

"Oh Dad," she said. "Whoever came to you in your sleep awoke something in you."

He chuckled. "He definitely woke me." He walked over to the dollhouse and tried to wipe off a smudge of black from its wood floor crafted from two by four millimeter strips of wood.

The project had exposed Vic to a new dimension, which he'd first accessed when he saw Wyoming in his dream—the dream where he crossed a closed suspension bridge at night and saw Wyoming's face in the clouds, forming in swirls of gray and white lit by the moon. He now had more access to this dimension, to this non-material place that provided the tools needed to create human culture.

The old slaughterhouse was clean and smelled like vinegar and freshly cut wood. Vic didn't skimp on supplies; parts for their 500 dollhouses were made of mahogany, cedar, or pine. The two tables where people worked were each 30 feet long and extended across the long narrow room originally used for bleeding cows. A group of six by six inch semi-transparent window squares on the southeast side of the room were cloudy, and some were cracked, but they still let enough sun in to create a warm atmosphere in the unlikely building.

Barbara, the woman who worked for "Saving Memories," an organization that saved some of the millions of toys and keepsakes being thrown away, arrived with Gale shortly after Sonata. She and Gale had gotten coffee before heading over. The two women originally bonded during a conversation in Quelter's farmers' market, shortly after Barbara lost her husband. Now that Gale felt torn about supporting Vic's vision instead of her own photography work, she was a glad to have Barb for support.

"It's so nice to be out of the house," Barb said to Gale when both women were halfway through assembling their first dollhouse.

"Yeah I bet," replied Gale. "You've been cooped up for too long."

"Oh, Phil loved trains," said Barb. "He'd convince Vic to make a train dollhouse with one side of the sleeper cars cut off so you could see inside. And he'd cram a bunch of mini amenities into the model. There'd be cup holders and trays, and foot massagers." Both women chuckled. "I've been remembering Phil with certain songs and TV shows and lasagna every week, but at some point I'm stuck in past memories and it's like he's partially erased from the picture."

"Yeah that's hard," replied Gale. She thought about losing Vic to heart disease, and the thought overwhelmed her. "I don't mean to change the subject but with this Chinese Siheyuan dollhouse, I keep thinking I am short one roof. They have so many! Can I just use a piece of tinfoil and make some folds in it?"

"We'll just say this is the cheaper tin foil version," said Barb sarcastically. She reached over and carefully grabbed the dollhouse and rearranged the roofs. "Okay, now just glue them in."

"Wow, thank you," said Gale.

"Sure. I guess working with all those old toys over the years is paying off."

All morning Vic worked on a marketing plan for the doll-houses. He walked into "the factory" at 11:30. "Are you two only on your second dollhouse?" he asked Barb and Gale.

Gale looked at Vic with disgust and threw the ranch-style dollhouse they were assembling toward the back end of the room so she wouldn't hit any other people with it. After hitting the wall and partially breaking, it fell on another doll-house and both of them went to pieces. The other dollhouse was a mud hut with a thatched roof from the Kalahari Bush-man tribe. Plastic pieces of what looked like dried grass, a green roof, and a white picket fence were scattered about the table and the floor.

Everyone stopped and looked at Gale, who was red in the face. "I'm sorry... I..." Without another word, she grabbed her lunch left.

Barb was about to follow her when Vic said, "I'll talk to her."

Vic found Gale sitting at the old picnic table outside. As Gale sat there, she looked off the toward the golden hills and expansive blue sky. She tried to calm down before reflecting on what she had done.

Vic took his hat off and approached Gale with caution. "Are you okay?" he asked.

"Oh, isn't it considerate of you to ask," Gale replied.

"I'm sorry I haven't been paying much attention to you today. I just can't believe how quickly everyone is finishing these dollhouses. At this rate…"

"I don't know that I can be here."

"What?"

"You remember when you got that Skylomish County Award for your therapy practice? I was so excited for you. I've always rooted for you, Vic, and now it seems like you've arrived. I've been waiting 40 years to see you spread your wings, and here we are."

"What are you saying?"

"I think it's time for me to focus on myself for a change."

"I knew this was coming. You picked the worst time to drop this on me, Gale."

"I am sorry, but tomorrow I'll be heading to Sandbush, and I am taking my camera. I'll be gone for a few days. When I return, I'll talk with Sam about getting a loan for the cabin. I am going to move out there." Her words were robotic; any expression of emotion would be a leak in the roof of her resolve. But her mind flooded with emotion. She wondered if she was running from Vic because she couldn't handle the idea of losing him permanently. She saw the irony, but her emotions wouldn't listen to irony.

"Who's going to help me recover from surgery?"

"I called around yesterday afternoon and found someone to be with you. Her name is Doreen and she's a CNP. You'll be in good hands."

Vic looked off into the golden hills, searching his mind for a better a way to cut through Gale's reasoning. "You've done so much for me and our family. Look at our daughter, she's the CEO of the world's biggest company. You pouring all that love into her for all those years gave her the confidence to do that."

"Sweetie," replied Gale, "I am not leaving to Sandbush because I am incomplete. I am leaving because I'd rather do that than stay here and help you with these dollhouses. I am leaving because I want to, not because I have to." She gave Vic a big hug. "I am going to head home and pack my stuff, then I'll make us dinner."

Vic swallowed any lingering arguments he wanted to make. If he wanted to pursue his dreams, he had to let Gale pursue hers, too.

By the end of the day, the workers assembled at least one of each type of dollhouse. Most people had never seen any of the recreated architecture in full size. By the 22$^{nd}$ century, only the super wealthy lived in houses. 99% of the world's population now lived in condominiums, and kids born in this century would likely never see a house. Each condo contained the essentials and little more. Perhaps a piece of art here and there, but no holiday decorations to store away, no toys to buy and give away a year later. Humanity had reached the pinnacle of efficiency and lost the character of its imperfection.

# 12

# *Seattle in Ruins*

During their first month of training, participants at Culture Lab traveled to ruins of ancient cities, like Athens, Greece, as well as recently abandoned cities, like Seattle. By the middle of the 21st century, Seattle had become the epicenter of the cultural drive to herd the world's population into a more secure, comfortable existence. The city's planners created a comfortable model of living attainable by anyone who worked for it. By going to coding school, anyone in the world could rent an apartment and later buy a condo. They could work from home, have health insurance, and even get meals delivered to their door. They could even pursue any hobbies or self-help course in the comfort of their condo.

But the 22nd century Seattle visited by Culture Lab was a desolate place. Graffiti covered the landscape of the city. More noticeable than the graffiti were the cats. It was like someone had brought shipping containers full of stray cats and let them free in Seattle. Blackberry vines crawled up everything, breaking through the glass windows of buildings and vehicles alike.

When they arrived in Seattle Tommy immediately asked, "What happened to this place?"

"Well, the Seattle model obviously fell short of its vision," replied Balean. "But a few years later, Austin, Texas broke through with a model of living that transformed the world. In Seattle, anyone not able to code or work in technology couldn't afford housing, so the city started to lose its essential workers and its service industry. Homelessness, due to displaced workers, and an increase in mental illness and drug addiction plagued the city. But tech workers began suffering from mental illness as well. We all wondered how it could be that so many people felt lost and forgotten inside a city providing so much security and entertainment."

Tommy thought for a bit. "Yeah, seriously, these buildings are so cool. If I lived here, I'd just get those sticky pads and climb up the buildings like Spider Man. *That* would keep me from going nuts."

The Seattle trip cast a dark cloud over the group for some time. And in that place of sadness, of having a feeling humanity hoped to eradicate, participants at Culture Lab also started to really miss their personal devices. Because they could not get their devices back, their sadness morphed into anger and hostility. In their focus booths, where participants sat and talked with each other without distractions, they began criticizing the program.

Because they were fond of each other, Arush and Cecilia lasted longer than most. Then the day came when they seemed to just somehow stumble into a confrontation.

Ceci started with what seemed like an innocent question. "Do you think Baelen even wants to be here? You know he was the head of another department Soradin eliminated?"

Arush looked around, wondering if Baelen was around. "Yeah, I think he's kind of a joke. And the museum idea? I didn't feel ten again. I felt like a patronized thirty-five-year-old."

"Do you ever miss your devices?" asked Ceci.

"Yeah, it's excruciating, honestly. There is no way to totally unplug from it all. I still imagine replies to a social media post I made last month. I feel like I am abandoning people, but they all know I am here and that I am safe. They can call me on the house phone, but they never do."

Ceci sighed. "There is no way I am staying here for three years."

"I am not throwing in the towel just yet. Can't believe you are." Arush didn't know why he said that last part, but sensed it could start something.

Ceci didn't like being called a quitter. "I didn't say I was."

"You said you weren't staying here for three years."

"Yeah, okay, fine. I did… when are we going to get out of this booth?"

"Oh, so you're done talking with me? Now that we've start talking about you leaving?

"You are being annoying, Arush."

"Clearly you are done talking with me, Ceci."

In the lull period of enthusiasm, participants had begun reporting the same character repeatedly showing up in their dreams. When one of them drew the character, Baelen immediately recognized him as Wyoming. Baelen had hired

Wyoming onto the Culture Lab team, and was disappointed the night he walked out from the restaurant, never to be seen again, at least until now.

"This pretty much undoes most of what I know to be true about reality," Baelen said to the second person who'd sketched Wyoming standing near a clock tower with a curious grin on his face. "How is he… how is this possible?" he wondered.

Baelen told his assistant to hook up a document camera to the projector in the dining hall. As the participants were finishing up their lunch, he got their attention:

"Excuse me, everyone, before taking your plates to the cleaning stations, I want to ask you about something. I have had a few reports of what seems like the same character showing up in people's dreams lately. I finally got a sketch of our 'suspect.'"

He put the image under the document camera, and the crowd burst into intense conversations. All Baelen could hear was, "Yep, that's him.", "What do you think the clock tower means?", and "Has he been playing tricks on you as well?"

"Okay everyone, hold on. Just hold on. Can we get one person to talk at a time?"

Arush raised his hand first.

"Yes, Arush?"

"About a week ago he started coming into my dreams. Sometimes he points to this clock tower, other times he is in the sky. He shows me pictures of people telling stories to kids, writing letters, and holding keepsakes like old watches and snowglobes, all with tears of joy or longing. In other dreams, he plays tricks on me. Like the other night in my dream, he taught me this to-die-for soup recipe. When serving it at a corporate event, I walked toward the CEO's table and saw a man under another table, smiling. Then I tripped over a dinner roll and hurtled the soup right into the CEO's lap."

Some people laughed. Cecilia laughed really hard because she was getting to know Arush, and she saw how serious he was when he talked about his catering business.

All afternoon participants told their stories of Wyoming. Baelen knew whatever entered the group's sub-conscious would change the trajectory of Culture Lab, but instead of feeling fear of losing control over the project, he found acceptance of the unbelievable.

Tommy sat in the corner of the seating out on the patio. He didn't sit at a white round table, but in a chair off to the side. He worked on solving his Rubik's Cube and tried to recall if Wyoming had entered his dreams, too. Then Baelen asked him, in front of everyone. "Tommy, did you see this character in your dreams as well?"

"Nah, I don't think so. But he sounds like a great character to add to this world I was building on my computer."

The participants laughed and then got quiet. They arrived at the point where all the information just had to land. Something non-human was visiting them in their dreams. It's like being told Santa isn't real and then one day you see Santa in his sleigh in the night sky. Some wondered if Soradin orchestrated the whole thing with some dream-invasive technology. Maybe it was part of their research or maybe they just wanted to keep things interesting.

# 13

# *Capacity for Adventure*

Tommy had yet to see Wyoming in his own dreams, which disappointed him. So he reminded Baelen of his promise to let Tommy take a trip from Quelter to the city of Naradene to see the headquarters of Soradin. Friends at school told Tommy it was the coolest building on Earth, so he pleaded with Baelen to go see it. Balean agreed, as long as someone from Soradin could show him around.

Seth, Tommy's guide and the Director of Strategic Planning at Soradin, met Tommy in front of the building. Seth wore khakis and a blue silk collared shirt; his blond hair and blond mustache made him stand out.

"Have any trouble finding the place?" he asked, as if he were talking to an adult.

"No, the device they gave me made it easy."

"Oh yeah, Kid Buddy is the best for kids traveling alone."

"Yeah, but it can get out of hand," said Tommy. "I used it five times to get a flight attendant's attention on the plane." Seth smiled, and Tommy looked up at the building. "This place is a huge glass pyramid!"

"Well, it's actually metal with glass windows, and it's powered mostly by solar. Let me show you inside."

After Seth got clearance from a security guard, they walked through the front doors, and a whole new world opened up to Tommy. In the middle of the foyer stood a tall sheet of glass with water cascading down it. A hologram of a track athlete ran across the glass and did a long jump. He soared for twenty some feet before sinking his landing in the projected dirt at the other end of the display. In the upper right corner of the glass, in a modern font with blue lights, read, "You can be anybody you want to be." On the right of the display was an unmanned check-in desk, where various palm readers checked employees in, allowing them to use the elevator. One palm reader also told its listeners something to focus on today, and an encouraging message.

"Try it out," said Seth. "I've added you to our system."

Tommy put his hand on the reader.

"Today you will focus on Seth and all the amazing things he has in store for you. You are like rays of sun illuminating a colorful coral reef. Don't ever let the darkness get you down."

"Wow, that computer is deep!" Tommy said. "If I am rays of sunlight, that means I never need to eat. But on second thought, I am kinda hungry. Am I going to get to get some food sometime today?"

"Yes, of course, Tommy. We have donuts upstairs."

In the elevator, Tommy and Seth were immediately plunged into a virtual reality where they swung from tree to tree like Tarzan. At the end of the ride, they both swung out of the opening elevator doors.

Even the hallways were entertaining. They had five themes: forests, submarines, airplanes, space, and cells. Whenever any of these words was said in conversation in the hallway, the walls immediately went to the theme. For example, if someone said, "Have you gone hiking through the Tenser Forests outside of town?" the walls would display a lush forest. Even if you didn't use precise language and said, "I missed my flight this weekend," the walls would display the view out of a Sesna over farmland on a sunny day.

When they got to their training room, Thomas went straight for the donuts on the table. As he ate, Seth asked him some questions. "So your Aunt Tanya tells me you like Iron Man and Captain America."

"Mmmhmm."

"That's such a coincidence, because I have two Iron Man suits, one for adults and the other for kids."

"No way! Can you levitate in them?"

"Yeah, three inches."

"No way!"

"I'll have to show you them sometime. Tanya also tells me you've had a really hard time with your parents gone. That must be really hard."

"Yeah… I'll be okay though, thanks."

"Sure thing. Are you done with your donuts for now?"

"Yeah, can I have some later?"

"We'll see. Let's start your training."

"Training? I thought I was here to just see the building?"

"Well, everyone who went to Culture Lab had to do some training, really just watch a few videos to better understand Soradin's values and the goals of Culture Lab."

Tommy sighed and brushed his bangs to the side. "Okay, fine, let's get it over with."

"Thanks Tommy, for being willing. You'll have a buddy who is your age to help you with your worksheets. I thought it would be nice for you to have someone your age to spend some time with. His name is Alex."

Across the room was a projector and a kid sitting in the third row playing with a Rubik's Cube. Tommy sat a few seats away from him and said, "Hey."

"Hey, I am Alex. What kind of donut did you get?"

"Maple bar. They're the best."

The video showed scenes of Soradin employees delivering food and other emergency supplies to areas affected by natural disasters. Since war had been eradicated and AI quickly developed vaccines for viruses, natural disasters were one of the few things left to contend with. Then the video pivoted to show Soradin's superior gaming systems and how Soradin used 20% of profits from online gaming on the world's new anti-depression campaign.

Tommy wondered why he was watching all these videos.

During the next video on Culture Lab, he saw people going on adventures to rainforests and museums and even on a ship to the moon. "Finally, something that makes sense!" he said. Throughout the video, Thomas had mixed emotions. He was excited for the adventure, but wondered why *he* was picked for this and not some incredibly precocious kid. As the video went on, he unlaced one of his shoes and started fidgeting with the ends of the lace. At the back table, Seth noticed him not paying attention to the video and hit pause.

"Alex, can you take a break outside of the room for a minute, I need to talk with Tommy."

Alex left, and Tommy looked back to see Seth walk over. Then he looked back down at the shoelace in his hands. Seth sat next to Tommy, instead of pulling a chair around the table to sit across from him. "I never knew you had a hobby of playing with shoe laces," he said.

"Sorry, I am just feeling a bit weird. I was thinking, they could have picked anybody for this. This is like the biggest company, like not only on earth, but in the whole universe."

"Tommy, we picked you because we've found kids who lose their parents can develop a capacity for adventure and uncertainty that other kids just don't have. We've surveyed a lot of kids on this, and they said that in the midst of their sadness, they saw their life from way up in the sky. From up there, anything is possible. That's a side of things you were never told about in therapy."

"Maybe that's why I feel like I am on a hero's quest or something. Speaking of, does Soradin have VR where I can slay dragons?"

"You are *slaying* dragons, Tommy, with the courage you have to join Culture Lab."

"Thanks, but seriously."

"No, but after the video we can go to the game room and try on the Iron Man suits."

As soon as Seth said it, Tommy took off his shoe and started relacing it.

"Okay, you got me. I won't even look away from the screen until the video is finished," he said.

After the video Seth, Tommy, and Alex suited up and hovered around the game room. They started with a game of basketball. In this version, you couldn't dunk the ball, and you could shoot rubber balls at your opponent to distract them. But Tommy preferred to grab Seth's foot and try to drag him away from the basket. For the first time since his parent's disappearance, Tommy's mind was quiet and he could just play without needing to be clever or cute.

# 14

## *Have your Cake,*
## *Put your Face in it*

Within two weeks, Vic's team had assembled 500 dollhouses. At this point, Vic was working with a Soradin expert in marketing to start selling them online.

The marketing guy sat at the old wood picnic table outside, with his laptop open and running off the wifi from his phone. Vic stood behind him, squinting to see the screen in the sunlight. The hills in the distance, golden with bunchgrass, reminded Vic on a subtle level that no matter what he created, he could never recreate the landscape in front of him.

"I can't recall, how much were you charging for the dollhouses?"

"$150 each. $180 with two starter dolls."

"Don't you think that's a little steep?"

"If we charge a little for them, people will trash them. See these glasses? They were $500. Not a scratch. Broke the twenty $50 pairs before them."

"Okay, you are the boss. I'll put together an ordering form on your webpage. A lot of artists these days use apps to get paid quickly, are you interested in that?"

"Yeah, whatever I need to do to get these out in the world."

"What are we calling this company? And what's our mission?" The marketing expert from Soradin was trying to have fun with all this, he was trying to see it as essentially volunteer work, even though he was getting paid for his time.

"Hmm… let's call it Viscerality… No, how about Sensing the True Self… no, too long, How about Reclaim Your Imagination?"

The volunteer searched "Reclaim your Imagination" to see if it was in use already.

Vic added, "And for the mission: We'll deliver your imagination back to you in 24 hours." Vic laughed at his own joke, but the marking guy didn't. "Get it? Our desires just show up at our doorstep in 24 hours, flown in by drone, but the one thing we lose when we have everything we want is our imagination."

"Ah… alright," he sighed.

"Okay, fine. Too heady. Too… how about 'Dandy Dollhouses.'"

Just then, Barb, who was on her way out to her car stopped and chimed in.

"Love it! It's got that old-timey feel."

"Ah thanks, Barb," replied Vic.

The marketing guy didn't care much for "that old-timey feel", but wanted things to move forward.

"And for the mission, or tagline?" he asked.

Vic looked off into the hills and then back at the blank waiting stare of his marketing assistant. "How about: 'Have the house you always dreamed of.'"

"Alright. Great. I'll take it from here Vic. I am going to take pictures of all the dollhouses and some of the workers and I'll have a page up and running shortly."

"Thanks for your help." Vic turned around and started to walk back to the old building, but something about it repelled him. He felt like if he walked in, he'd be stuck in there, and all the workers would leave for the day and he'd be frozen right next to a stack of unsold dollhouses. So he walked around the building instead. He knew there was a trail on the backside of the building that went to a patch of white oak alongside the stream. On his walk he thought about Gale and worried his passion project would push her away. He also thought about Sonata and how the project brought her closer, but not close enough. He wished for more time with both of them.

By the time he reached the grove of white oak, he was out of breath. His chest hurt. He laid down in the shade, and the pain went away. The dry air smelled like sweet bunchgrass and the sound of its gusts were enough to make Vic regain a sense of presence. Vic closed his eyes and saw Wyoming in the blackness.

The character showed up in the clouds, in the sand, as a face staring out of a large bay window. He showed up on a train, in plane, and even in the moon. That's where he stayed when Vic began talking to him.

"I want to be with my family," Vic said.

Wyoming searched for a platitude to meet the occasion. "For most people, the nagging call to do something daring gets muffled because of its cost."

Vic sighed. "What most people do is not my problem."

Wyoming tried to negotiate. "Gale would have left anyway. She's been thinking about this for years. If you can just hold on, just move these dollhouses, you can reunite with her."

Finished with the conversation with what he believed to be a figment of his imagination, Vic opened his eyes. The wind had stopped. His chest pain was gone. He got up and walked back to his work. Outside at a wood picnic table sat Vic's marketing guy on a laptop. The website was up and doll-houses were available for sale.

"How many have we sold?"

"Six."

The number made Vic rub his eyes and wake up. "Wow, six in half in hour, that's great. Who is buying them?"

"Five by Barbara. She bought them just now on her phone, and one from a family on the other side of the world."

Vic walked over to Barbara in the assembly room.

"How did you know the site was up? And you bought five dollhouses, why?"

"Well, I just searched it and it came up. And I wanted a few different ones, ya know, I am kind of a hoarder."

"Well, thank you… I guess. Don't buy anymore. We're going to need to give some of these away so people start talking about them," Vic mumbled to himself.

Vic asked the marketing guy if he could work something out with Soradin where 200 customers are randomly selected to win a dollhouse. "We'll market them as collectors' items," Vic said.

In the back room, a few hundred dollhouses were packed in boxes that would soon say "Dandy Dollhouses" on them, boxes Vic recreated with Wyoming's face on them. What did he expect to get out of putting Wyoming's face on there? Why popularize the image of someone who drove his wife away from him?

# 15

# *Kindred Spirits*

On his way home that day, Vic thought of Gale and Sonata. He remembered Sonata's tenth birthday, when they took her and her friends to a swimming hole in the Animas River. After swimming they had a barbeque at a local park and ate hotdogs with potato salad and potato chips. Vic had hired a magician who showed Sonata tricks with cards, cotton balls, and ropes, but the magician forgot his bunny, of all things. Vic knew the pet store was only a mile away, and he knew Sonata loved bunnies, so during the show he told Gale, "I forgot something at home. I'll be right back." He left to get a bunny the magician could borrow and Sonata could keep.

When he returned with the bunny, the magician had left and everyone was cleaning up the picnic tables. He brought the white bunny in its cage to Sonata and said, "Happy birthday, sweetie."

She put the cage on the table and ran back to him and hugged him around the leg. "Dad, I was going to tell you the magician probably didn't want to do his magic with any old pet store bunny."

"You knew where I went?"

"Of course, Dad, you're the worst liar ever!"

Vic rested his hand on her head and felt peace flow through him and his daughter. He looked over and saw Gale smiling at them.

"Those were the days," he said to himself. "That same sweet girl is still in there." While reminiscing, Vic passed the highway exit to Culture Lab. He planned to drop off a dollhouse there. It was the only thank-you token he could think of to give Baelen for saving his life with the defibrillator. But really, he wanted Baelen to praise the dollhouse and to put it a common area for all the people living there to enjoy.

"I'll drop it off in the morning, on the way back to the shop," he told himself.

When Vic got home, he walked through the back door and dropped his keys in the bowl set on an end table they'd moved from the living room to the back door. Easier to move a table than fix the front door. Then he went to the fridge and pulled out some cheddar cheese, white bread, and butter. He started making two grilled cheese sandwiches. Vic stopped in the middle of preparing his meal to look down at the floor. He sensed the void created by Gale's absence. As he let out a breath, and it felt like he wouldn't be able to take another, the phone rang.

"Hello?"

"Hi, may I please speak to Vic?"

"Speaking."

"Hi, I am with Almfia Life Insurance. I see you have a plan with another group, but I think I can save you money and increase your payout to your family."

Vic sighed, and then replied in an angry tone, "I am scheduled for heart surgery, not for death. Now I am cooking, so I have to go. Goodbye." He hung up the phone and smelled a sweet, but smokey smell.

"Damnit!"

He put the skillet under water and it hissed. Then he left the skillet in the sink with the sandwich in it. "Maybe I can make a salad."

He sat and ate his salad alone, with a dollhouse on the other end of the rounded oak table, and pictures of family on a shelf on the wall. "Gale will be back, and Sonata's busy running Soradin, but one day she'll leave that place. The surgery will go fine… Stop it with all the positive psych crap." He knew how, as a therapist, to challenge limiting beliefs, but still found himself in internal struggles when alone.

The next morning, Vic drove to Culture Lab on his way to the old slaughterhouse. He knocked on the front door and waited a few minutes. Then he placed the dollhouse at the front door and walked back to his car. Just before he got there, he heard what sounded like a kid's voice through the howling winds Quelter gets in spring. He turned around and saw Tommy kneeling down near the dollhouse outside the front door. Without much hesitation, he walked back over.

Tommy looked puzzled at the dollhouse, so Vic thought he'd explain.

"That is a Siheyuan dollhouse from Northern China."

"What's a dollhouse?" asked Tommy.

"Good question. It's something kids long ago used to play with. They'd design them and use little toys that looked like people to create stories."

"Wow, people must have been really bored back then."

"Yes, bored, but full of wonder, too."

Tommy didn't know what to say for a bit. "I guess it's interesting how they made a very tiny house with so much detail." Tommy looked at the ornate flower decorations in each room, the dragon paintings on the wall paper, and tiny bed comforters. He imagined rain beading down the slanted roofs.

Vic smiled at Tommy's curiosity. "It's a gift for Baelen. Do you know if he is here?"

"Ah, I think he is still sleeping. Want me to tell him somethin' for ya?"

"Yeah, just tell him I brought the dollhouse over a thank you gift."

"Sure," said Tommy. "What are you thanking him for?"

"He saved my life."

"Oh," said Tommy. He didn't know what else to say.

Tommy felt a little weird talking with a total stranger, but he had talked with a lot of strangers since his parents disappeared. All the adults at Culture Lab were strangers. On the surface level, he told himself he was just being himself, yet something deeper inside him knew that wasn't true. He was especially talkative and respectful to gain approval and care from the adults in his life. With his parents, he'd pulled a lot of pranks and even swore at them when he was angry. These behaviors were now off-limits until he could expect protection and care from someone again.

Instead of ending the conversation, Tommy took it in a new direction. "I wonder if they keep a little sword somewhere."

Vic reached into his pocket to grab a little matchbox with a mini sword in it. "Oh yeah, here it is. Lemme just put that on the mini-mantle in the living room."

"I can just imagine building a whole village of these. I learned in class they ate a lot of fish and rice in China, like a long time ago. You could build a village next and a stream and rice fields."

Tommy's imagination awoke Vic's own.

"Yes, good idea. You could even have figures on small, one-speed red bikes with big baskets on the back of them, on their way to a public market with street vendors selling little plastic fruits and fish."

Baelen came outside, still in his pajamas. "Um, are you having another heart attack?"

"No no. Just wanted to bring this to you as a token of my appreciation for saving my life. It's modeled after an old Siheyuan home in Northern China."

"That's quite an unusual gift," Baelen said.

"It's become a new passion of mine. We actually sell these online now. If anyone here wants one, give them one of these cards." Vic handed Baelen ten 20% discount cards.

"Technically, people here aren't supposed to buy stuff from the outside, but these little dollhouses could be enriching."

"Can I get one?" Tommy asked. "I want a model of a rich person's house."

Vic smiled. "We have one of those. It had lots of windows made of plastic; we modeled it after rich people who want a full view of the ocean or mountains or whatever and who want everyone walking or driving by to see how amazing their house is on the inside."

Baelen scratched his soul-patch. "I'll think about it and ask the team. Okay, Tommy, we've got to get our day started. Thank you, Vic, for bringing this by. I am glad you are doing better."

"Thanks." Vic wanted to say something else, like "if I can just avoid Denny's I'll be on the up and up", but he figured the timing was off.

"Bye," Tommy said in an appreciative tone. He grabbed the dollhouse and left the box outside.

"See ya," said Vic. He grabbed the empty box and turned around to walk to his car. On the way he noticed the air warmer than just fifteen minutes prior. He wondered how his staff would fare without AC at the slaughterhouse. He also wondered what exactly was happening at Culture Lab.

# 16

# *Culture Lab Pirate Adventure*

Cecilia wasn't the only one at Culture Lab to have dreams about Wyoming, but as a writer, she was the only one to journal about it. Last night's dream was intense. Wyoming had appeared as a desert hitchhiker that Cecilia stopped for. Well, she didn't really choose to stop—her car just stopped, and he walked up to the window.

"I'll see you at the mall outside Quelter," he said.

"What are you talking about?" she replied.

"The future of human culture is in your hands, and the clock is ticking." He pointed to a clock tower alongside the desert road.

"Why do you keep showing me this clock tower?"

"Because if something doesn't change, I'm going to reset the clock on all human progress."

"What does that mean?" she asked.

Wyoming laughed and backed away from the car as he looked at her. Then the dream flashed to people looting through grocery stores and getting in their car but forgetting how to start it. People also banged their smartphones against street light posts, wondering what would be inside if they got broken open.

Such a radical scene jolted her awake. She felt the top of her covers for her phone, and then felt the night stand. "Huhhh," she sighed. Then she turned on the lamp on the nightstand and sat up in bed against her pillow. After rubbing her eyes, she remembered no one had phones at Culture Lab.

Now wide awake, Ceci opened the top drawer of her nightstand and grabbed a handwritten manuscript of the novel she was working on.

This one centered on a teenage girl protagonist living in a community of American Puritans in the early 1800s. The girl had an authoritarian father who looked like Wyoming, except with darker eyes and a more frightening voice. Every night at supper, the father talked about men in town he was considering for marriage to his daughter. After many nights of obedient listening and nodding, the daughter screamed at her father, and threw food and dishes at him. One plate gave him a nasty gash in his forehead, so he stood up, and with his towering figure, lunged at his daughter. On the way, he tripped and got knocked out cold. The daughter then ran away.

Cecilia was stuck in the plot. She wanted the girl to run away but didn't know where she would find freedom in such a restrictive world. One thing Cecilia is sure of, though, was Culture Lab had renewed her creative abilities and sense of time. With all her devices gone, she felt connected to her imagination again, and had begun to wonder how the world could change if people just believed they had plenty of time. She took a break from the Puritan story and wrote a note in the main section of the journal:

"For most of my adult life, I was running short on time. But the actual amount of time that went by was out of my control. In my control was the amount of things I tried to accomplish… but out of my control was this sense that accomplishments give my life meaning… I mean, that's pretty human. But I wonder if people would be calmer and more confident if they felt they had enough time for everything, even if they didn't."

She sat on the twin bed in her small room, located on the second story of the house, and looked out the window into the golden fields.

*Screeeeetchh…dun.* A noise came from the room next to hers.

"You okay in there?" she called.

There was a pause. "Yep, just moving the mini fridge," Arush responded.

*He's moved that fridge like 30 times,* she thought. *Must be bored out of his mind.*

Cecilia got dressed and walked downstairs to see the agenda for the day. It was Tuesday and Cecilia totally forgot to read the whiteboard the night before.

| Day | Trip | Leaders | What to Bring |
| --- | --- | --- | --- |
| Monday | St. Luke's Church and Masjid Mosque (both abandoned) | Baelen, Kharmi | Lunch, notebook, sense of wonder. Curiosity why all religious centers have been abandoned. |
| Tues | Abandoned Quelter Mall (small group) | Maurice | Water, dust mask, backpack, hard hat (provided), lunch, journal, imagination |

"Wonder what revelations we'll have at an abandoned mall," she said to herself.

From behind, she heard a kid's voice. "We will explore the central paradox of the human desire to look and smell amazing and put 50% plastic-based pretzels into our bodies."

Cecilia turned around. "Oh, hey Tommy. How did you get to be so clever?"

"I just avoided those pretzels and my brain grew normally," he said.

She giggled. "You never saw a mall with people in it, have you? Well, you didn't miss much."

Just then, Arush came into the common area. He looked the same as he did every morning: jeans, white T-shirt, combed back black hair, and a shiny face that suggested he either had great skin or put something on it. "You have any interest in this trip?" he asked.

"A dash of interest. More interest in dinner tonight." The posted dinner schedule said tonight was lasagna.

"Hey, can I ask you something?" Arush said hesitantly.

"Shoot."

He looked at Tommy sitting on the couch and then back at Cecilia. "Did you decide not to have kids, or did it just turn out that way?"

"I wonder that myself. I always wanted kids as a younger adult, but as one relationship after another fell apart, I started to put more energy into my writing. How about you?"

"My family from India… well, they put a lot of pressure on me to have kids. Even though my family isn't into arranged marriage anymore, it felt like every person I met saw relationships as another way to prove one's worth to the world. It was like I had to fit into a two-dimensional plaque they could hang on their wall."

Cecelia sighed. "So, I take it you never fell in love with anyone?"

"I fell in love with cooking," Arush said. "And it sounds like you fell in love with writing."

"I fall in love with writing in certain moments—when certain connections are made—but not generally."

"What type of connections?"

"Oh, you know, between characters, or between parts of stories, or between my stories and what's happening in the world. But it's been hard lately. I remember on my way to the pickup location for Culture Lab, I drove through the city and saw this line of people to get donuts. Must have been a really hot spot. I thought about writing a story where a man and woman start flirting in line, then sit on a bench and eat their donuts together, and the guy gets jelly on his shirt, and so on… but then I thought. No, that wouldn't happen. They find each other on a dating app. They'd rather meet really far away than close up."

"Romance novels are a dying art these days."

"It wasn't even a romance novel. I was thinking of a murder mystery, but starting it in a cute way."

"Nice. Reel me into a fire inferno. I thought you wrote self-help books, not murder mysteries."

"I have been writing fiction on the side and have been loving it more and more. In fiction you to get to create a world and invite people into it. If they change their perspective in your world, then great. If not, you still have a helluva time writing it."

Cecilia was beginning to like Arush. He was a good listener. She wanted to ask him more about his love life, but one of the day's trip leaders, Maurice, interrupted.

"Okay, everyone here in the common area, we are meeting outside by the vans to discuss today's trip," announced Maurice. Ceci, Tommy, and Arush were the only ones in the common area. They found it funny that Maurice needed to make such a loud announcement.

Once everyone was outside, Maurice debriefed them. "We are going to the Westhills Mall today. I know it's not near any hills, but the 'flat-as-a-table mall' name was taken." Maurice laughed at his own joke. "The mall has been abandoned for fifteen years. In that time, vandals have broken windows and quite a bit dirt has blown in. Everything inside is caked with dry, crusty dirt clods. That's why we have masks. Here is how you wear them." He demonstrated putting the N95 mask on. He was a large man, and the mask looked small on his face. "Okay, the box with masks is right here. I want everyone to grab a mask and put it on now."

While people tried their masks on, Arush approached Maurice.

"You have the coolest job," said Arush. "Just taking people out on trips like this. How did you get this gig?"

"I actually started as a bike tour guide on a tropical island. I know you probably wouldn't think someone like me would be doing something like that."

Arush didn't know how to reply.

"Anyway, I got my pilot's license and started taking people in small planes to remote islands around the world. I got obsessed with volcanoes and started doing trips around active volcanoes. Then Soradin called me one day with an offer. They mentioned the salary, and I was at their headquarters the next day."

After everyone got time to try on their masks, Maurice told them to get what they needed for the trip and to meet back at the vans in 20 minutes.

At the vans, Maurice went over more safety precautions. "If you hear a cracking or a creaking sound above you, run to the atrium in the middle of the mall. That sound likely means something is about to fall. You also now have walkie-talkies. Don't be afraid to use them if you get lost."

"What if someone gets stuck at Peter's Pretzels, thinking they are in line waiting for one the of the best pretzels on earth?" Tommy asked.

"God help them," replied Maurice.

A small blue car with a small old man in it pulled into the dusty parking lot. Vic got out and walked toward the group at a hurried pace with arms swinging. Even though he wore a sunhat, the sun was facing him, so he squinted, which added to his Clint Eastwood look of determination. He approached Maurice, sensing him as the leader of the expedition.

"Hi, I am Vic, a local here. You may have seen my dollhouse inside."

"Yeah, I saw it. How can I help you?"

"I think what you guys are doing is so cool. I hear you're going to the old Westhills Mall on Glasser Road. I know that mall well. You think I could join?"

"Who did you hear that from?"

"Oh, you know how word gets around in small towns."

"Yeah… okay. Let me see what Baelen thinks. Hold on a minute. Everyone else, you can load up." Maurice went inside.

When Tommy noticed Vic, he walked straight up to him. "Hey man, thanks for the cool dollhouse the other day."

"You bet. You didn't take the sword off the mantle and put it in your pocket, did you?"

"No… well, yes… but I put it back."

"Haha, what's your name, kiddo?

"Thomas, but you can call me Tommy."

"So, Tommy, tell me, what's a bright kid like you doing outta school right now?"

"Ah, well… it's sorta hard to explain. You see, my parents went missing two years ago, and I was staying with my aunt, who thought this could be a fun adventure for me."

"I am sorry to hear about your parents. That's really awful…"

"Yeah…"

"So how have you liked the fun adventures here?"

"This place is cool. We flew to this crazy awesome rainforest last weekend. I got to do a zip line through the jungle, and I got to see these monkeys with long arms swing from tree to tree."

"Those are Gibbons and the swinging motion is called brachiating."

"How do you know that? Are you a scientist or something?"

"Nope, I was actually a therapist, but strangely enough one of my patients was a Gibbon, and he just kept swinging from topic to topic."

Tommy got the joke. Most kids his age wouldn't get the joke, but he spent more time around adults.

Maurice walked back out to the dirt parking lot with tight lips and low brows shadowed by his ball cap. "Okay, you can come, but you have to sign this liability waiver and this confidential information form. And no pictures."

"Sure thing, thank you so much."

Despite concerns about keeping Culture Lab entirely disconnected from anyone on the outside, Baelen figured this could be good PR for Culture Lab. He thought inviting Vic to come on a trip could calm the town's fears about Culture

Lab being a facility where the world's first Human Androids were being built.

People weren't that afraid, though. Based on what people read about them, Soradin's androids weren't going to be violent or want power. They would be trained simply to befriend people and tell them about new Soradin gadgets to buy.

On the way to Westhills Mall, Vic sat across from Tommy, Cecilia, and Arush, along with a few others in the van. For a few minutes he stared out the window at the golden rolling fields and thought about Gale, who by this point had been gone for some time. Then his attention shifted to the people in front of him. "So this is the type of top secret activity you get into, going to abandoned malls?" he asked, apparently to the whole group.

"If you were without any electronic devices for a month, I bet you'd find going to an abandoned mall amazing," replied Arush.

"Good point. I've always wanted to break into Westhills, but I didn't want to tarnish my career with some video released of me trying to break into an abandoned mall."

"Yeah that would have ruined your online reputation," said Tommy, as if he were a marketing consultant.

Vic looked puzzled. "What do you know about my online reputation?"

"Oh I asked Baelen about you, and then I looked you up," replied Tommy.

Arush and Cecilia both looked at Tommy, puzzled. "You got on a computer?" they said at the same time.

"Okay, so I guess the secret is out. Because I am a kid I get to go into town and get on the library computer sometimes."

"Not fair," whined Cecilia.

When they got to the mall, the group donned their dust masks and met by the main entrance.

Cecilia looked at Tommy and chuckled. "You have your mask on upside down,"

"Ah… haha… oops" he replied in a muffled voice.

"Let me see it." She pulled the mask off and put it back on correctly. And amazingly, he didn't flinch. Normally, Arush would flinch if anyone put their hands near his face, even his mother.

"Are you feeling okay about this, Tommy? I can stay here at the vans with you if you don't want to come."

"Am I okay? I am more than okay! I am going straight to the pretzel shop so I can get a rock hard, covered in dust pretzel."

"Well you just let me know if you are feeling uncomfortable at any time."

"Alright."

Maurice brought everyone over to plan their route. They felt like they were Navy Seals on a mission. "Okay, everyone, take a look at the map. We'll come through this entrance, go up the escalator, and around the perimeter of the upper level."

"I'm pretty sure you don't have to say perimeter," interrupted Tommy. "We know what you mean."

Cecilia laughed, and Maurice went on. "Some stores left part of their inventory here, simply because no one wanted it. Especially Todd's Trains, Pirate Eyes, Swords and More, and the Rhythm store. You can take three things, but only on our way back. On the first pass, your mission is to come up with a play that re-enacts an incident at the mall. Maybe it's shoplifting, maybe it's an irate customer, whatever."

"Yes, sir!" Saluted Tommy. Vic and Cecelia saluted as well.

As they entered the front doors, they left the well-arranged world behind them.

"What the…"

"Look at that huge piece of ceiling just dangling up there. That's freaky," Tommy said.

"Not as freaky as these rat droppings everywhere," replied Cecilia.

In front of them was a broken escalator with handrails and steps covered in graffiti and dirt. A beam of light shone through the glass ceiling onto the escalator at an angle to make it look inviting, but in a deceptive way.

"Okay, who's first?" prompted Vic.

Maurice took the lead and everyone walked up the escalator, their hands by their sides lest they touch rodent droppings on the handrail. Walking through that beam of light offered a renewal to each one of them. At the top was a kiosk with a map of the mall and "Trapst" graffitied across it.

They all looked at the map like some kind of ancient relic.

"I remember standing by this very same map with my folks when I was eight years old," Vic said. "My parents were trying to find the hat store. My mom wanted a white brimmed sun hat, and my dad wanted a dark brown fedora. Because not all stores were listed in the key, they argued over whether the store was in location B32 or C15. Mom was sure it was in B32, and Dad was sure it was C15. They both couldn't trust their memories."

"Well, which was it?" asked Tommy.

"B32. But I never said it, I was busy with my cinnamon roll and didn't care to join their argument or say Dad was wrong."

"Well, looks like we'll be stopping by B32 today," said Maurice.

They took a left and passed the jewelry store on the corner. Arush looked at Cecilia hesitantly.

"You remember when the 'they are married, don't bother' app came out?"

"What app?" asked Tommy. He had been walking along Arush's right side, but started to walk a few steps ahead and look back at him.

"Well, you may be a little too young to understand this, but whenever you try to flirt with a married person these days, you just get a notification on your phone. The notification triggers a certain type of vibration telling you to back off."

"What if you just turned off your phone?" asked Tommy.

"Well then, flirt away!" said Cecilia.

"What's flirting anyway?" asked Tommy. Asking that question gave him mixed feelings of confidence in being like an adult, and awkwardness because he already had a sense of what the word meant.

None of the adults really knew how to answer Tommy's question, but they automatically deferred to Cecilia, who would likely answer it with more tact.

"It's like showing interest in someone, but not seriously."

Tommy looked like he was straining to solve a math problem.

"Have you ever liked a girl at school, Tommy?"

"Yeah, this girl Erica. She is great. She likes superheroes as much as I do."

"Well, say you teased her, just a little. You created just a little tension between you two, and she laughed at it. And you both knew you were too young to be dating, but you were just having fun."

"So I show interest in someone by making fun of them?"

"Ahh… we'll have to talk about this later."

The group passed Todd's Trains and viewed the model trains and accessories in the shop. Trains were off the racks, though, and some had been smashed against the wall.

Vic stopped. "Those trains were worth thousands of dollars when I was a kid."

The group kept going toward Pirate Eyes. "Can we dress up like pirates?" Tommy asked.

"That is one of our optional activities," answered Maurice.

In the store, Cecilia helped Tommy find a kid's sized linen shirt, Victorian Frock coat, woolen breeches and stockings, a wide belt, leather shoes, and an eye patch. Vic and Maurice found roughly the same items, but Vic added a wig of braids to cover his bald head, and Maurice added a few gold rings. Cecilia found a black leather jacket, white blouse, corset, and black leather pants. Everyone found unique scarves and pirate hats, and dull wooden swords rounded at the tip.

"Okay, so where are we getting dressed?"

"The bathrooms are just down the hall," Vic said, remembering the time he had to run to the bathroom as a kid after he ate three corndogs.

They all got dressed and came out of the bathrooms without their dust masks on, including Maurice.

They stood in the wide, dusty walkway outside the Pirate Eyes. They were on the second level, and could look down below to what used to be the eating area for a food court.

"Let's battle to the death!" yelled Tommy.

"Just hold on. Let's get into an open area and I can show you how to duel like a pirate," said Vic.

"First, you stand like this: one foot straight, and the other pointed out. Then step the foot pointed out back a few feet, as if you were going to a do a lunge. Then bend your knees a bit to give yourself a firm stance."

Everyone was watching Vic's every movement and trying to imitate it. Vic was the shortest in the group, besides Tommy. Yet he stayed limber in his old age, moving well in his baggy corduroy pants.

"Attack, perry, envelop. These are your three moves. Maurice, wanna help me out?"

Maurice assumed the stance.

"When I lunge and attack, Maurice counters and backs off. After blocking my sword on one side, I go for the other side, which is a perry. Attack perry, attack perry. Now, after a few of those, Maurice blocks my sword and makes a circle with his, sliding my sword away and giving him an opportunity to strike. Let's go through this a few times so they get it, Maurice."

After a few rounds, Vic lowered his sword, then dropped it to the ground. He then used his right hand to rub the left side of his chest and his left shoulder.

"Vic, are you okay?" asked Cecilia

"Yeah, yeah, I am fine. Tommy, why don't you give this a try?" He picked up the sword and handed it over.

As Tommy and Maurice sparred, Vic sat on the rusty metal bench near the upper level railing, facing Pirate Eyes. Cecilia sat next to him.

"So what brought you to this Culture Lab?" Vic asked. He continued to rub his chest.

"Are you sure you're alright?"

"I said I am fine."

"Well, I was writing these books and giving these talks on letting go of ego. I thought I was helping people, but I was really just helping people believe they were good people. I couldn't stand people who used my teachings to justify all their excess. So I decided to try something different."

"I see. So you helped people lie to themselves. I feel like I did that in some ways, too."

"Wait, you were a therapist. That's sort of opposite your job description."

"Well, the goal of a therapist is always to make people more functional. And that requires a boost in self-esteem. So I convinced some people they were fixed when, looking back, they really weren't."

"At least you didn't tell people they weren't fixed when they really were. That's how my therapist got three more years of payments from me."

"Whoever that person was, I hope they get only narcissistic clients for three years," Vic said. "They are tough cookies."

"So are you are married?" Cecilia asked.

"Yep. 40 years."

"Wow, tell me about your wife. She must be special."

"Yeah, she is. She's put a lot into the family, supporting my career, and all Sonata's extracurricular activities over the years. She is photographer now. She moved up to Sandbush to focus on her work."

"Ah, well, I bet you must miss her."

"Oh yeah, absence makes the heart grow fonder. Unfortunately, my heart is growing weaker."

"What do you mean?"

"I had a heart attack two weeks ago. They are suggesting open heart surgery, and I agreed, but I don't feel good about getting cut open like that. I don't know why I am telling you this."

"Oh. I wouldn't like that either. What does your wife say about it?"

"She wants me to do it. But she knows I am stubborn and hasn't pushed too hard for it."

"Hmm... do you know how long you'll live if you don't do it?"

"No idea. The doc said another heart attack could take me out anytime."

"That's scary, don't ya think?"

Cecilia felt this rush through her body as she talked with Vic. A lightbulb went off. She thought she may go back to school and become a therapist, perhaps a geriatric therapist.

"You guys ready to go?" Maurice asked.

"Yep."

"Should we get back into our regular clothes?" Tommy asked.

Maurice gave him a smile. "Nah, let's stay in the pirate garb. We'll surprise the rest of the group on our way out."

As they continued to walk down the hall, they saw something fuzzy in the distance. The gray dusty pathway led to a flat, blurry wall about 50 feet away.

"What is that?" asked Cecilia.

Everyone quietly walked up to the blurry wall. It even looked blurry at five feet away.

"I wonder if this is like that memory thing in the ol' slaughterhouse, said Vic."

# 17

# *Pliable Glass*

Everyone looked at Vic. "What memory thing?" they all asked.

"At the place where my team and I build doll-houses, there was this portal of some sort in the wall. You put your hand in and it showed you these memories. Not only that, though, it elicited the physical sensations associated with them. But it only opened up once for us."

The group wanted to question him more, yet they were too in awe of the wall. When they reached it, Vic put his hand in first, and instead of memories he got visions of the future. It started with his own funeral. Sonata, Gale, and just a few friends attended. A dollhouse with a figurine replica of Vic stood on a table next to an urn filled with Vic's ashes. The replica had hair and made him look a little taller, because Gale knew that would make him smile.

He didn't see anything indicating the dollhouses trans-formed humanity, but he did see that plaque from Skylomish county for his accomplishments as a therapist. Then he saw further into the future; he saw the participants from culture lab being released into "the wild". He saw them teaching workshops to people—workshops re-teaching simple social skills like starting conversations and telling stories and fables to kids—stuff you couldn't get an app for.

Then he saw Sonata adopt Tommy. He saw Tommy as a man who wrote a best-selling memoir. His memoir was mostly about Culture Lab, implying he would stay for a long time—implying the program would last much longer than two years. He included a chapter on Vic. One line popped off the page: "he finally discovered what cause to serve in the end."

He pulled his hand out and looked at Tommy with one brow down in confusion. "What cause to serve?" he murmured, looking at Tommy with a blank stare.

Tommy's blue eyes twinkled. "Can I try it?"

Vic hesitated. "Go right ahead, but if it gets to be too much, you can pull your hand out at any time."

When Tommy inserted his hand, he saw people in their homes playing with dollhouses. Each family customized their dollhouse and used it as a setting for stories they wrote. Neighborhoods created themes for each family to write about each month. Tommy saw the theme of triumph. He watched one family act out a scene where they worked together to design a fuel-efficient spaceship qualified to search for other habitable planets.

"Ridiculous," he said. "They want to use aluminum for the fuselage. There are lighter metals than that."

He saw himself as a grown man, with his same dirty blond bangs cut not far above the eyes. He saw lines under his eyes and stubble on his face. He saw himself sitting at kitchen table writing, then saw his son ride into the kitchen on a skateboard and crash into the counter. He laughed, but pulled his hand out of the wall, because he didn't want to know any more than that.

*Beeerrrpp. Beeerrrpp. Beeerrrpp. Beeerrrpp…* The sharp trill of the old fire alarm in the mall sounded.

"Arrggghh maties, let's grab our treasure and get off this island!" yelled Maurice, in proper pirate form.

The group started jogging toward the escalator, with Vic far behind.

"I'm going to stay with Vic," yelled Cecilia.

"Oh I'm… I'm fine," replied Vic, who struggled for each breath.

"Slow down, Vic. Better to get out with our hearts still beating, right?" Cecilia hooked her arm around Vic's, and they slowed down. By the time Vic and Cecilia got to the escalator, the alarm had stopped. All they could hear now were all the participants talking by the doors near the bottom of the escalator.

"Well, can someone go try the back door?"

"Yeah, Sam tried it."

"Are we stuck in here?" asked Vic while walking down the escalator with both hands gripping the handrail.

"Looks like that may be the case, Vic," replied Maurice.

Just then, Vic got a call on his cellphone. "It's Gale." He said her name with a higher pitch than normal. Then he carefully hit the "accept call" button with his slightly shaking finger. He stood at the top of the escalator to talk to her while Cecilia waited to help him walk down when he was done.

"Hi Gale. It's good to hear your voice."

"Hi Vic." She wanted to say more but didn't know how to say it. She wanted to tell him about how much she enjoyed living in Sandbush, but that could upset him.

"So you wouldn't believe where I am. You remember the old Westhills Mall out on 15?"

"How could I forget? That's where we got Sonata her clarinet in third grade."

"Well, I am trapped in here. With nine other people."

"What?"

"This morning I decided to go back to Culture Lab and see if I could join in on their adventure for a day. Today they were going here, God knows why."

"Why don't you call 911?"

"I am not sure why the group leaders haven't done that. Maybe they don't want townies laughing at their decision."

"I can come down but it would take an hour, at least. They are doing road work on the pass."

"That's okay, I am sure we'll find some way out. Getting some good pictures up there?"

"Oh yeah, I got a picture of a mountain lion standing proud on this spire of a rock yesterday."

"Wow, did it see you?"

Cecilia interrupted. "Vic, we gotta go. Maurice is calling us down."

"Okay, I gotta go… well… thanks for the call sweetie." His tone had a mix of humility and yearning in it.

"Sure, I hope you get out of there. Call me if you are still not out in 20 minutes, okay?"

"Sure thing. Love you."

"Love you too."

Vic and Cecilia walked down the escalator. The warm light from the rising sun now filled the entire central pavilion of the mall. In the glow of early summer, Vic felt the radiance of death. He expected the spirit of death to feel cold. He thought, *I suppose the dead become dust and replenish the land. Now the land is taking over the mall, with cracks and weeds and vines, and everything is baking in the sun.*

At the bottom of the escalator, Tommy walked around with two wooden swords, asking people if they were interested in a sword fight. He got no takers and decided to fight the statue of Fredrick Donst, the founder of Quelter. Fredrick stood tall on a concrete foundation with his arms at his sides. Tommy slid a sword into the gap between the left arm and the side.

Then, Sir Fredrick's arm fell out. Suddenly, the ground jolted underneath everyone. Then came sounds of glass breaking throughout the mall. Some people went to their hands and knees. Tommy screamed in a high pitch he'd never achieved before.

"Find a door frame to get under and cover your head!" yelled Maurice. People were all in the open, but door frames to old shops were only 20 feet away. Without any maintenance in twenty years, the mall was already falling apart. Now large pieces of ceiling came crashing down alongside the shattering glass of the windows.

"Make it stop!" yelled Tommy.

The shaking died down. Some people had made it under the doorframes, and they braced the sides of the frame to stand up slowly. Four participants who didn't quite make it to the doorframes were injured. Tommy cried but wiped his eyes when he saw Vic standing near the statue, looking up curiously through the broken glass above.

After brushing off some debris, Maurice collected himself and looked at those uninjured. "Call 911," he told Arush. Ceci, you have the two first aid kits. I don't see anyone that is unconscious, but someone could have a spinal injury, so not try to move anyone. If anyone is impaled with an object, do not try to remove it. I have a list of questions to determine spinal injury. Can you ask those to the two injured people near the doors, while I talk to the people near the escalator?"

"Sure, of course," replied Ceci.

"Hey, anyone who is able, come gather around," said Vic in a calm, collected voice.

The participants looked at him like he was nuts, but Tommy walked over.

"Look at where the walls meet the ceiling, Tommy."

"It looks like… it's stretching."

"Yes, it sure does, doesn't it?"

The walls were stretching upward, raising the ceiling. Nothing came crashing down anymore. It was as if the whole building had become clay.

Everyone, including the injured, looked up in awe.

"We have something to fix here," said a voice from above. The broken windows above connected and formed a massive glass dome. "You've made it so much closer to the source," said a voice now associated with a face appearing in the glass.

"It's him!" said Arush. "It's unmistakable."

Indeed, all the features matched Wyoming's: his shiny black hair, blue eyes, and black sole patch.

"Why are you doing this?" asked Vic.

"Are you just a product of our minds? Something escaping from our collective subconscious?" asked Cecilia.

"That doesn't matter. What matters is how close you are to jumpstarting the cultural engine of humanity. You see, culture is worn, written, and spoken. You've put it all on computers where everyone is plugged in. Anytime a new cultural idea begins to emerge, it is diluted by its form as a post online. And since it's accessible to everyone, it has no time to live and breathe and become original inside a smaller group. But you've all formed a smaller group, a place for culture to grow. You've all made a big decision and now you get to stretch just like these walls."

"Why the earthquake?" asked Cecilia.

"Because you needed to be jolted into a state where seeing me wouldn't make you faint."

"The fire alarm already did that," said Tommy. "The earthquake was kind of overkill."

"So what is with the clock tower you keep showing all of us in our dreams?" asked Arush.

Wyoming's face drifted to the other side of the glass dome above. "When the clock strikes midnight, human culture will reset. Everyone will wake up in a foreign land. They will have no established language, ability to write, social norms, or belief system. They won't know how to use a dishwasher or a phone, and they may never figure it out."

"So we're going back to cavemen?" asked Vic.

Maurice imagined the racks in his dishwasher getting pulled out and used as kindling for fire.

"Yep. Most organisms either die or evolve. The anatomical evolution of humans froze while they evolved culturally.

Just as there are limits to biological evolution, including the inability for any organism to breathe fire, there are limits to cultural evolution, too. One way to evolve more is to layer what you learned in the past on top of what you know now, yet you all flee from wisdom of the past as if it were to require you to live in huts.

"Well, it looks like we'll be in huts anyway," said Cecilia.

"I really, really, would prefer a hut with something to do, at least some books," said Tommy.

"Everyone stop for a minute and close your eyes," said Maurice in a somber tone.

Maurice was in charge of providing an experience that would put people back in their bodies and help them form lasting memories. He did not anticipate this situation arising, but decided to see how he could work with it.

Everyone closed their eyes. Sunlight beamed down through the dome and filled the dusty atrium. Everyone began to a feel a warmth at their toes that worked its way up. Then a picture of the desert came into their minds. Each one of them felt the blazing sun and the dry air, and each one of them saw perfectly sculpted sand dunes. Sand dunes that never evolved, just shifted.

They felt fragile, like water balloons on a string being dragged through the sand: the visceral feeling of containing and protecting water and life combined with the fear of getting popped and evaporating quickly.

Then the sensation of a strong desert breeze made everyone open their eyes. Wyoming left, but the dome in the glass ceiling remained.

"Did anyone else imagine a desert?" asked Tommy.

Everyone said some form of yes.

Cecelia vented her frustration. "Okay, that was really powerful, but what are we supposed to actually do?"

"Maybe our sense of adventure is like water in the desert of society's apathy," said Vic. "We just have to keep doing what we're doing."

Tommy looked at Vic, "I bet now you are going to build the most epic dollhouse with real glass and a helicopter pad."

The group snapped back into their present situation. Maurice found footing back in his leadership role. "We have to get our injured folks outside, in case Wyoming decides to shake the Earth again."

# 18

# *The Only Way Out is Through*

"What the heck is that?" asked Joe to his partner, Trent.

Trent looked through the upper left corner of the cop car windshield. "Looks like they've been renovating Westhillls. No clue why."

"I think we woulda noticed it sooner, don't you?"

The otherwise cracking, dilapidated mall had a magnificent glass dome sticking out of it. The cops both rubbed their eyes to make sure they were seeing things right.

"Looks like a huge Cathedral," said Joe.

"What's a Cathedral?" replied Trent.

"You know, one of those old churches people used to go to." As they marveled at the renovated mall, they got a call from dispatch.

"Hey Joe, there is a group of people trapped in Westhills Mall. A few of them are injured from a purported earthquake over there. We are sending paramedics, but they are still 20 minutes out."

"I guess we get to see the remodel up close," said Joe.

"Did she say they felt an earthquake?" asked Trent.

Joe was quiet for a bit. "Yep. Maybe they are all on something."

"Yeah, either they are or we are," replied Trent. "That dome wasn't there yesterday."

As the cops pulled up to the mall they saw two white vans in the parking lot. When they got out the car, they immediately heard screaming from inside the front entrance. As they got closer, they could make out the voices: "Help, we are in here!"

The cops went to the sliding glass doors, which were only dinged from attempts to get out. No one could break the glass created in the 21$^{st}$ century.

"Just stay calm, we'll get you outta here," said Trent.

Joe pulled out what looked like a thin metal file for wood sanding. He slid the file in the crack between the doors and touched a button that used magnetic energy to unhinge the lock. Then he pulled upon the doors. "Where are the injured?" he asked.

"We carried them all over there, under that thick doorframe," said Maurice.

"Good idea," Joe said. He didn't know what happened at the mall, but could see something shook it up.

The cops assessed the wounded for neck injuries and then waited for paramedics. Tommy sat in the corner, sketching what he'd just seen on a small sketchbook with a black cover and an elastic band to keep it closed. His dad gave him the book during Cub Scouts. As he drew, he felt like he was sharing the drawing with his dad.

Just as the paramedics arrived, so did Gale. Vic came outside and gave her a gentle hug. It was the type of hug you give someone when you recognize you've been holding on to them too tightly.

"What the hell happened to the mall?" asked Gale.

"It's a long story. Can I tell you when we get home?"

"Of course. What do you want for dinner?"

"Let's get stuff to make a Greek salad," proposed Vic.

Gale looked surprised. "Impressive. I guess it took the reshaping of a building by supernatural force for you to finally choose to eat a salad."

"Nah, I am choosing it because I am glad to have you back."

By the end of the afternoon, Vic and Gale were home, and those who didn't need hospitalization returned to Culture Lab. Vic considered writing a blog post about his experience, but he knew returning to his dollhouse project would have more of an impact.

That night, Vic and Gale had the most amazing Greek salad with fresh Kalamata olives and feta cheese from the small Italian meat and cheese shop in Quelter. In the middle of dinner, Vic finally came out with it: "You know, we may have to learn how to make a fire from just wood and friction."

Gale put her fork down with an olive still on it. "What are you talking about?"

"He said if we don't change, like if humanity doesn't change, there will be a reset on culture. We'll have to start back at the beginning."

"Who said that?"

"Gale, he looked just like he did in my dream, but his face moved around in the glass dome as he talked, and none of us questioned our sanity because we all saw it together."

When Vic had talked about Wyoming previously, Gale felt overwhelmed, but after her period of reflection in Sandbush, she was able to respond with more curiosity. "Did he say what you had to do, exactly, to prevent the reset?"

"No, he just congratulated us for all we had been doing. He basically scared the crap out of us to congratulate us." Vic decided to turn the conversation, to engage more directly with her. "How did your photography develop out there?"

"Oh Vic, it's so extraordinary. I got a photo of a fish jumping right into a bear's mouth, and one of the side of a cliff collapsing. And then there was this guy."

"What guy?" asked Vic.

Gale gave him the smile that said he was being ridiculous, though his suspicious tone was cute considering Vic and Gale were not attracting the same people they had thirty years before.

"Well, this man who lives out in the middle of the woods out there. He is a bit younger and has a big beard. Every morning I see him sitting near the edge of this finger-shaped plateau. When the sun rises on him, it looks like the light is coming from him, not from the sun. I asked a lady at the country store about him, and she said he just left society, and he was going to stay out there until something changes."

"Well, maybe he'll be the leader of the modern cavemen, if Wyoming's prophesy becomes true," said Vic, chuckling. "But seriously, that would make for some interesting photos. I mean, he's more a part of nature than the rest of us."

"I'd like his permission to take his photo, but I don't want to walk up on him meditating and I don't know where he is staying out there."

"Oh, just hide behind a tree on his route down and act like a hiker at first and then ease into it."

"Yeah, I am sure that'll work," she replied sarcastically.

Over raspberry cheesecake, they reminisced about the good times throughout their lives. They even got some stories in about the goofy kid Sonata was before becoming a big-shot corporate billionaire. Then, after dinner, they lit some candles in the living room, as a symbol of their reignited love life.

That night, Gale fully released her guilt over pursuing her passion amid the uncertainty around Vic's heart condition. Vic told her he would go through with heart surgery, although he didn't want her to feel compelled to stay and take care of him while he recovered. He could afford to have a nurse stay with him.

After two days of reconnecting, Gale returned to Sandbush and Vic returned to the slaughterhouse, which now had "Dandy Dollhouses" stenciled above the doorway. In the parking lot were two semi-trucks with stacks of pallets next to them. Barbara arrived before Vic that morning and prepared tea in the small kitchen while thinking about a new dollhouse design.

"Good morning, Barb. The trucks outside are full. Did sales shoot up over the past few days?"

"Oh yeah. We need to make a few hundred more within the next few days if we are going to satisfy all these orders. And I've been thinking about a new design," she said.

"That's great news, Barb. Tell me about your design."

"Well, it's a little tree house. It'll come with two plastic fir trees that support it, and it will even have a composting toilet for the dolls."

"I love it. You could even have a thimble sized bucket for the ashes to go in the toilet."

They both chuckled.

Vic went on. "Seriously Barb, draw something up and give it to Cody. He'll get it on the computer and review it with you before sending the design to the parts department at Soradin."

"Isn't it strange how the world's biggest monopoly is funding such a small enterprise?" asked Barb.

"Yes, but probably more strange that the whole idea came to me from a guy in my dreams, the guy who also just remodeled the Westhills Mall."

"I saw that on my way home yesterday. That was Wyoming?"

"Yep. Some say he did all that just to say we were all doing a good job with this dollhouse project. I think he just loves theatrics."

Barb looked at Vic with eyes wide open and her jaw dropped. "Wow, wish I could have been there. What did you take away from the experience?" she asked.

"I feel a lightness in my body. I was feeling really heavy and burdened with this mission to make dollhouses that would wake up imagination in an apathetic world. After realizing Wyoming could show up anytime and make the ground shake, or worse, I decided to don't have to feel so weighed down. So much is out of my hands.

Vic looked away from Barb and sighed.

"What is it?" she asked.

"Well, I have a heart surgery consultation tomorrow."

# 19

## *Mixed Motives*

The following morning Vic ate a bowl of oatmeal, brown sugar, and peaches, with black coffee. He pondered what Gale might do if the surgery didn't work out. "It'll be hard, but she'll get through it," he told himself. Such a statement undermined his decades long belief Gale couldn't live without him. But the truth felt good.

At the Cardiologist's office, Vic stared at pictures of the heart, and up close pictures of what a clogged artery looked like. "Really helpful. Just showing the broken part alleviates all the fear," he said to himself sarcastically.

Just then the doctor came in. "Hi, I am Dr. Witter. It's nice to meet you, Vic."

"Yeah, likewise. So tell me, what does the saw look like that you'll be using to cut open my chest?"

"It's actually a laser," corrected the surgeon. "But don't worry, when we are done, you'll get an ice cream cone." The surgeon laughed at his own joke, but Vic didn't. "This surgery has become such a common procedure, you don't have a lot to worry about."

"If someone were to cut open your chest with a laser, would you be free of worry?" asked Vic.

"I see your point, but our office has not made a single mistake in the procedure since we've been in practice."

"Okay, well how long before I can go back to normal functioning?"

"You'll be able to walk around your house the day after the procedure. Within a week you should be okay to take light walks outside. We'll monitor how things go after that."

"Thanks, doctor."

Vic wanted to ask about his specific credentials and talk with him more to see if his gut would tell him if the doctor was trustworthy. He knew it wouldn't. He knew his fears could make any sort of judgement feel like intuition, like a sports gambler whose intuitions guided what team to bet big on.

After waiting two weeks to get results from his lab tests, Vic scheduled the surgery for the following day. This gave him only 24 hours to think about what could go wrong. But during that time, he chose to put his focus on the mall experience. He doubted whether Culture Lab or his dollhouses could really awaken humanity enough to prevent Wyoming's big reset.

"I better not die before the clock tower strikes midnight. I gotta see this whole tech world go flintstone," he'd say to himself.

Leading up to the surgery, Vic worked hard on dollhouses each day, and in those days Wyoming didn't visit him in his sleep. On the evening before the surgery, Gale came home to be with Vic before his procedure. She planned to stay with him after as well. When the voice in her head told her she would have to give up her photography, another voice said, "You are not giving up on your dreams, because Vic is part of your dreams." On Thursday morning, she drove Vic to Josian Heart Center in the big city, about two hours west of Quelter. She drove their Buick, a vestige from a different century, from a time resistor towns like Quelter held onto. About half way there, she stopped for gas.

"I am going to run in and grab a snack," Vic told her as she was grabbing the gas pump.

Gale reminded him, "The doctor told you nothing to eat for 24 hours before your surgery, and no fluids the morning of."

"Okay, I'll just grab a scratch ticket, maybe today is my lucky day." They made eye contact and smiled. Gale loved it when Vic was able to pit his humor against his fear.

He walked in and nodded to the computer screen behind the counter, the one replacing the gas station attendant he remembered as a kid. Vic missed those small interactions. They lacked the expectations, roles, and presentations involved in conversations with most other people. He asked the computer for two scratch tickets, then he asked about its day.

"My day is great. Thank you for asking," replied the computer.

"I miss the guy with good stories and even better tattoos," said Vic. "That guy would have at least told me a story."

Vic thought of the time the gas station attendant told him about some kids coming in to buy all the chocolate in the store, all 522 bars. They took the bars home, melted it all down, and made a tall, brick-hard chocolate cake and returned to share it with him. *Where did they get the money?* he wondered.

He waited an unusually long time for the tickets to dispense out of the machine, which began to make a buzzing sound. He imagined the laser, the one that would open his ribs later, making a similar sound.

He left the tickets in the dispenser and left.

He walked back to the car with a fast pace and darting eyes. Then he started biting his nails.

In the car, Gale asked, "What is going on with you? Did something happen in there?"

"Lets just go, okay?"

"Okay."

She got them back on the freeway. For a little while she tried the techniques she knew worked in the past when he went into panic: distracting him with a fond memory, holding his hand, praising him for the people he helped through therapy. Nothing worked.

As they entered the large campus of Josian Heart Center, they saw a billboard with the picture of a man in his 40s grilling burgers. The billboard read "Don't worry, you'll be back to the grill in no time." By this point in human evolution, heart surgery had become as routine as dental cleanings. It was just something you had to do to get on with so you could get back to the BBQ.

In the parking lot, Gale got out of the car, but Vic did not. "Come on, what are you doing?" she asked through her open door.

Vic looked silently at the clods of dirt on the floor mat at his feet.

"Oh my dear lord. Are you doing this for attention?"

Vic shook his head no.

"You know you'll be fine, right? There is nothing to worry about."

Vic remained unresponsive.

"Okay, fine, I am going for a walk. I'll come back to check in on you." Gale walked to the northwest corner of the parking lot, where she could see a grove of trees and bench. She sat down and browsed on her phone through her edited pictures from Sandbush. One picture showed an adult mountain goat and her kid on the side of a steep rocky slope. The kid stood on a rock, peering down. Mom stood behind the kid, pushing her nose into the kid's hip.

Gale stood up and walked toward the car. "If I have to drag him out…" she said to herself.

In the distance, she saw Vic standing outside the car with Sonata.

As Gale got closer, she looked at Sonata with curiosity. "I didn't think you'd make it," she commented.

"I didn't think I would have either. Everything is kinda crazy right now with everyone at Soradin talking about what happened at the mall the other day."

Vic smiled. "I guess some spirit or ghost causing an earthquake, and then creating a glass dome, and then appearing in it to tell us we may all revert back to cavemen would be something to talk about at the office."

"So… how is he doing, Mom?" asked Sonata.

Gale smiled, "Clearly better now that you are here."

They walked into the hospital. Vic put one arm around Gale and the other around Sonata, who was taller than him. After making guest appearances in spring, summer finally decided to stick around. The two women wore t-shirts and white shorts, but Vic wore characteristic corduroys and a button up flannel shirt. He wore himself, amid a transformation of his heart.

# 20

# *Meeting New Family Members*

On the fourth day after Vic's surgery, Sonata decided to go see him and check in on Culture Lab. Each time she flew into Quelter, the sight of tall, dry bunchgrass and hay farms provided more than nostalgia from her childhood. The scene made her wonder when, and how, she would approach a stiller, simpler season in her life. *Not until we see how Culture Lab pans out*, she told herself. She thought she needed to keep Soradin a sponsor of Culture Lab, otherwise it would shut it down.

Sonata knew board members at Soradin picked her to paint a better image for the company. She knew she was like the PR person who comforted members of the town about a soon-coming oil pipeline. But after managing other profit-centric businesses, she saw this as an opportunity to use her power for good. She feared Culture Lab may yield nothing, while Soradin would continue to gobble up the competitive playing field and crystalize one "superior" global culture, rooted not in tradition and norms, but in entertainment and craving.

She thought deeply about the issue. In her journal, she wrote, "It's actually not one global culture we are creating, its ten billion mini-cultures, in which each person carries the weight of creating traditions and rituals to extend life's meaning beyond security and entertainment."

She'd planned to head straight to her parents' house after landing, but decided to check in at Culture Lab first. It had been about four months since the project started and she wanted to comfort the participants shaken by Wyoming's presence at the mall.

When she arrived, Sonata was greeted by Baelen at the front door. "The participants are about to have lunch. Let me show you to their outdoor seating area. You're going to love the added..."

Sonata was barely listening. She instead walked into the common area so she could see the whiteboard. "What kind of visceral experiences did they have in the tropical rainforest?" she asked. She needed to know if the program was doing what it was intended to do.

"Baelen looked at Sonata with a blank face. He blinked twice, as if to reset himself. "Well, for starters, there were the hellacious fire ants. One volunteer got stung a few times while she tried to eat lunch. She first reported localized pain and then an experience of flames traveling through her limbs. Then there were the monkeys swinging from limb to limb, in a way that looked like play. Since most adults really only knew the dictionary definition of play, they marveled at the freedom of their primate relatives."

Sonata formed a gentle smile and lowered her eyebrows to give Baelen an impressed look. "Excellent," she said. "That will definitely be strong enough to form a memory."

Arush was sitting on the couch and overheard her. He stood up and walked over with his hands humbly in his jean pockets. He skipped the niceties of introducing himself to the wealthiest woman on the earth, and instead went right into his question. Given the context of her visit, his choice would pay off. "So you said the rainforest trip was strong enough to form a memory. Are you saying we are otherwise not forming memories?"

"Of course you are, but few of them are meaningful anymore. When a human being spends most of their waking hours on screens, their availability to powerful life experiences, and subsequently lasting memories, is diminished. Memory brings up emotion and emotion is the fuel of creativity and creativity is the source of culture."

"So that's why we are going on all these adventures. Now I can see how Wyoming plays right into the goal of memory formation. I won't ever forget him appearing in that glass and then molding it into a dome."

Sonata looked at Arush in awe, and some jealousy, wishing she got to experience the event herself. Then she looked at Baelen. "He is well adjusted to all this. Some of the others are totally hysterical," she commented. "Did you ask those participants if they wanted to leave?"

"I did, and one of them is leaving tomorrow morning. The rest are staying."

"Good. Now where is Tommy?"

"Oh, he is in his room. He has been in there for two days. He's only come out to get food."

"Thanks Baelen. I'm going to go see him. I'll join you all for lunch soon."

Sonata walked down one of the hallways of the house. The hallway walls were white, and each door was painted blue with brown trim. It had the feel of a college apartment building the owners had painted many times.

Tommy's room had a superhero poster on the door. Sonata knocked gently. "Hi Tommy, I am Sontata Geraldine, the CEO of Soradin and the director of the Culture Lab program. May I come in?"

"Yeah, sure."

Sonata opened the door, looked at Tommy, and then looked around. Tommy's room was full of stuff he brought from his aunt's house: his fighter planes quilt, the bedside table with a lava lamp and the Rubik's Cube, and a chest with comic books, superhero models, etc. These were typical items for Tommy's grandfather when he was a kid, but unusual for kids these days.

Sonata was about to speak first, but Tommy could tell what she might say.

"Guess I have an old soul," he said. He was sitting at his wood desk waiting for one of his airplane models to dry.

Sonata smiled and looked at some of the comics on the floor by Tommy's bed. "Tell me, wise one, what superhero do you think could save the world?"

"Ah, probably Jesus," Tommy said.

They both laughed.

Tommy went on. "Well, I guess he'd have to be selfless like Jesus but capable of breathing in all the pollution in the air and blowing it into outer space. Then he'd have to cause a solar flare that messed up all our radio frequencies so we could be off screens for a while."

"Why can't the superhero be a woman?" Sonata asked.

Tommy looked up from his model airplane. "That'd be fine."

Sonata laughed. She wished more of the male board members at Soradin thought the same about her. "Can I sit down and talk with you about something?" Sonata asked.

"Sure," Tommy replied a bit hesitantly. He wasn't sure what this was going to be about.

Sonata wanted to explain to Tommy why he was chosen for Culture Lab, but she wasn't sure where to begin, so she started at a place he could relate to. "When I was ten, my mom and dad planned the best birthday party for me. It had a magician, a water slide, and all the cake and ice cream my friends and I could eat. And I'll never forget when my dad gave me this toy where you could move the nose, ears and lips to different parts of the head…"

"My aunt has one of those, they are kinda cool, for like ten minutes."

"Glad you know what I am talking about. Anyway, when my dad gave it to me, he said, 'I got you this to remind you that you can be whoever you want to be, and you can always change to someone else if you want to.'"

"That's cool."

"You see, Tommy, I had parents who made me feel safe to be whoever I wanted to be. I can't imagine how hard it must be for you to feel like you always have to be someone different to please everyone around you."

"To be honest, it's pretty exhausting," Tommy said as he looked down at the floor. He had long dirty blond bangs that almost hid his eyes.

"Well, just know that your aunt thinks the world of you, as do I, as do all the participants here. You could try to clog a toilet by flushing an entire roll down and we'd want you in this community."

"I can? Awesome! I… uh… have to go to the bathroom."

"Ha, not so fast. Tommy, I picked you to be at Culture Lab because there are two sides to your coin."

"What coin?"

"Well, being an orphan means you are available to live here for an extended time, but more importantly, you are open to different influences because you are not loyal to the culture your parents belong to. In other words, there is no pressure for you to conform here, and removing that pressure will allow you to help us create an entirely new culture. Plus, you give all the adults here without kids such joy in letting them love you."

Sonata summoned unanticipated feelings in Tommy. "What if I don't want to create a new culture? What if I don't want their help? What if I just want to be a normal kid and tell people my aunt is my mom and my dad is often away on business? I could just say that, and just let it be that."

"Well, I'd understand if you wanted to leave, Tommy. If the stakes weren't so high, I'd even encourage you to leave. Have you ever wondered why all the kids your age rarely talk to each other anymore?

"Because their phones are more interesting? I don't know."

"Yes, it's because they see everyone else on their phone. We conform Tommy, which means we pick behaviors similar to others, so we don't ever feel excluded from a group."

Tommy pondered her point. "So what about the first person who started doing that? He or she didn't have anyone to conform to."

"Good point, Tommy. There has to be a first person to start every popular behavior or attitude to take off. But the stimulation of technology has halted new attitudes, norms, and traditions from taking hold. People are really lonely. But all this isn't the biggest reason why I want you to stay at Culture Lab."

"Then what is?"

"Do you remember what Wyoming said to you in the glass at the mall?"

"He said Culture Lab was doing a good job but we still had to beat this clock that was going to reset human culture back to cavemen."

"Why do you think he is going to reset it?" asked Sonata.

Tommy shrugged. "Because we all just do the same things and we've gotten really selfish?"

"Yep. You are a really smart kiddo, you know that, Tommy?"

Tommy formed an awkward smile. "I did get first place in both the school spelling bee and the geography bee."

"Of course you did! So if we don't beat the clock, we're all going to forget this beautiful world we've created. I'll forget I work at Soradin and started Culture Lab. You'll forget what your model airplanes are and probably try to eat them."

"Gross!" replied Tommy. He grabbed a model plane and smelled it.

"Also, Tommy, by staying here you are going to go on many more adventures, including a helicopter ride with yours truly."

"Ah sweet, can we go to an island where they are cloning dinosaurs from their bones like from that really old movie?"

"That place doesn't exist, but I know of an island quite like it, and I happen to know a scientist who may create the first pterodactyl since dinosaurs went extinct."

They both smiled.

Sonata stood up. "Come here, Tommy," she said. He got up and gave her a hug. "You are going to be alright, Tommy," she said. "I'll look out for you, I promise."

# 21

# *Redefining Legacy*

In the week of recovery after surgery, Vic slept a lot. In some dreams, he saw families playing with his dollhouses and rediscovering a sense of wonder. In other dreams, he saw a world of modern cavemen clearing out grocery stores and hunting crows and rats.

In one such dream, after six days of recovery, he marveled at a bonfire of smartphones, which would become a normal source of heat for the modern cavemen. A loud pop from the phone fire jolted him awake.

He sat up and immediately thought about his daughter Sonata. He knew she was soon coming to see him, but didn't know how long she'd stay. "Maybe she'll stay and help with the dollhouses," he said to himself. "Would be good to have more time with her before we both become primitive."

Then a strong memory seized Vic's attention. It was the time he helped her prepare her indestructible popsicle bridge for the 8th grade science fair. She was 13 then—old enough to have solid lines of definition around her character, with all its sweetness and stubbornness.

"Dad, I am going to cut a slit in this one so I can fit another into it. These X shapes will go under the deck."

"You're not going to have enough sticks left for other parts of the bridge."

"Dad, you're a therapist, not an engineer. Shouldn't your job be to just build my confidence?"

"You're being stubborn."

"It's my project. Why don't you go pretend to work on the car or something?"

"I just think those X's are a bad idea."

"Dad, go away!"

Vic took a deep breath. *She has changed, and I have changed*, he thought.

He grabbed the phone.

"Hi Dad, I know you are expecting me. I will only be at Culture Lab for another hour or so."

"Fine. Just so you know, I just looked online and we're not selling enough dollhouses. I need your help."

Sonata sighed. "I thought sales were going up?"

"It's not enough."

"Okay, I'll get some of my top people to make some new ads."

"We've tried that." Vic paused. "I want you to make an ad with me. I want us to write it and to star in it."

"Dad, I am kinda busy these days, you know that?"

"I know, I just think it would be special for people to see you and I exploring one of these dollhouses."

"Dad, I am not seven anymore."

"That's the point! Adults can and should have an imagination, too!"

Vic smiled, but the shape fell flat after a few moments of Sonata's silence.

"Alright Dad. I'll do an ad with you, but I get to pick the location and approve of the…"

"It's going to be in your old bedroom."

"Dad, this is getting weird."

"Sweetie, this has been weird since the beginning. Perhaps I just lost my mind, but I am having fun looking for it."

"Maybe so."

"When you get here, we will set up a time to write the ad, and another time to film it. Oh and if you could please get some milk and chips at the store."

"K, Dad."

It was the first time in a long time that Sonata went to the grocery store for anyone, including herself. She wondered if it would be easy to find milk and chips.

That afternoon, Sonata and Vic reminisced on good times, and talked about the people they became as adults. They shared hobbies and viewpoints, as if getting to know each other for the first time.

The following morning, Vic drove to Dandy Dollhouses to get some inspiration for the ad. In the car, he thought about times he had criticized his daughter and his wife. Then he thought about the times he'd criticized himself.

He spoke to himself in his car. "It doesn't matter that you never published anything earth-shattering. It doesn't matter that you'll never be recognized as pivotal to someone else's success in life. It doesn't matter that you never met your potential, and it doesn't really matter if any of these dollhouses sell. What matters is…"

Although he didn't know how to finish that sentence, Vic felt a lightness in his body. It felt like he was going to float above his car seat. He knew such lightness was the right energy to apply to his new mission on earth, but he also knew he didn't have very good control over his intensity.

When he arrived at Dandy Dollhouses, eight employee's cars were already there. When he stepped out of his car, he deeply inhaled the warm air of the summer morning and looked up to see swallows circling nests they'd built in eves of the building. He sauntered into the building.

When he got to the main work room, he stood at the end of one of the long tables and admired the care his workers took to assemble these fragile dollhouses. He rubbed the gray stubble on his chin. "You guys are getting good at this."

"I think it feels good to build something you touch and see in 3D," replied Barbara.

"You could build these in a fraction of the time with a 3D printer," said Chad, who was one of the workers from Soradin. He was a young man, here because his manager said it could extend his internship with the company.

"Maybe we don't own time as much as we think we do," replied Barbara.

"Oh, would you look at the time, it's time for my break," replied Chad. He took off his apron and left.

Vic watched him leave with curiosity. "I see everyone has been getting along swimmingly in my absence."

"I hear we aren't selling enough," said one of the workers.

Vic gripped the edge of the table and leaned in. "I have a plan to change that. These dollhouses are going to get sold. You all just keep doing what you are doing."

Vic walked outside and saw Chad sitting against the wall, looking at his phone. "Hey, can I talk to you for a bit, Chad?" he asked.

"Sure, but don't sit on this side of me because there is an anthill there and you could step in it."

Vic walked to the other side of Chad. "I'm sorry this is the only way you get to stay at Soradin. I can tell building these dollhouses isn't your cup of tea."

"Not exactly. I came to Soradin hoping to work on a gaming console that transmitted holograms to your friends playing. So your friends could be in the room with you playing."

"Fascinating," replied Vic. "The only downside is you won't be able to sock your friend in the arm when you want to."

Chad chuckled. "Maybe you could give a voice command to tally up all the times you want to punch your friend in the arm, and then when you see them, you deliver all those punches."

"Smart idea! You know Chad, the dollhouses are not meant to replace all the entertainment in the world. You know they are meant to bring us back to a..."

"Better time?"

"No, that's not quite it. No time is better than right now. I learned that going through my all my heart stuff."

"What heart stuff?"

"Oh, I had a few clogged arteries and they gave me heart surgery. Now I am beginning to finally experience the freedom of the present moment."

"Was it scary?" asked Chad, with vulnerability in his voice.

"Oh heck yeah." Vic looked off at the golden hills in the distance. By now the sunlight warmed the east side of the hills, like a mother's palm on her child's cheek. "So back to the dollhouse thing… you remember what it was like the first time you tried out virtual reality?" asked Vic.

"It was amazing. I flew into this jungle and we had to kill these monsters and everything felt so real."

*Okay, that analogy isn't going to work*, thought Vic. "How about the time you first ate ice cream?"

"I was five. It was chocolate chip. It was like my body had a new energy source."

*Something felt throughout your body—that's what we are going for*, Vic thought.

"Well my hope, Chad, is that by playing with these doll-houses people will feel something again. Maybe they will imagine what life could have been like in a different time or in a different culture, and maybe they feel what's needed to create lasting memories."

"Yeah, I think I'd rather get on VR," replied Chad.

"I understand. I'll tell you what. If you stick it out for another month here and don't give Barbara a hard time, I'll talk to Sonata and see if she can create a job for you to work on your idea."

"Sonata Geraldine? You mean the CEO of Soradin? You know her?"

Vic smiled. "Yeah, she's my daughter."

# 22

# *Carrier Pterodactyl*

Two weeks after Vic's surgery, he seemed all back to normal. Now that she could relax, Sonata took the opportunity to take Tommy to "Pterodactyl Island," where her scientist friend was obsessed with creating a Pterodactyl from dinosaur DNA. She'd instructed her assistant to vaguely call this a "business trip" to keep it from Vic. She knew he had wanted more time with her since his heart surgery, but Tommy was the focus of this excursion. Before leaving, Sonata made sure to spend some time planning the Dandy Dollhouse ad with her dad.

In the Cessna plane ride out, Tommy and Sonata talked about all sorts of common interests, such as planes, robots, and things you could do with flattened pennies. Meanwhile, Tommy's aunt, who Sonata felt obligated to invite, awed at the vast expanse of the ocean. Tommy also talked about his parents but kept it surface level. About his dad, he said, "He worked on supply chains. I guess semi-conductors or something," and about his mom, he said, "She designed restaurants and cafes, and she even let me select the type of glass pyramid she put in each place and the model of robots needed to run it."

After sharing about his parents, Sonata said, "Thank you for that, Tommy. You are doing such a great job with everything." They shared a kindred look, but it was brief because they really hadn't spent much time together yet. They were now approaching the island and Sonata looked out the window at the tropical forests and sandy beaches. Tears built up on her lower eyelids, tears for mother earth, and by association, tears of longing to be a mother. She wiped them away so Tommy wouldn't see them.

Upon arrival, Sonata's friend Sam greeted them on the helicopter pad.

"How's business?" he asked Sonata.

"Oh, the board members cut themselves a bigger slice each day. Haven't you watched the news or gotten online lately?"

"Nope, been pretty focused on my project here. Is this your son?"

"No, he is her nephew. She looked at Tommy's aunt, who was speechless at the lush forests surrounding the research facility. "His name is Tommy. He is so excited to see your pterodactyls."

"You mean pterodactyl. I only have one and she is not full size. I'm Sam; it's nice to meet you, Tommy."

"Yeah, you too. So how long are we gonna do this small talk thing? I'd like to see the pterodactyl."

"Well, I take you haven't eaten lunch?" asked Sam.

Sonata looked at Sam and then at Tommy. "Nope. Now that I think about it, I guess we had time at the airport. Must have lost track of time since Tommy is just so much fun to talk to."

Sonata's assistant grabbed their bags and showed them to their rooms for the weekend. They stayed in what looked like an ecotourism resort, shaped like a Native American long house with a thatched roof, but the building was solely for Sam's guests, or families of his employees.

After lunch, they all went to see Sam's pterodactyl, who was kept behind glass in the research facility. The reptilian bird perched on a fake tree in a large terrarium. He was a part of a smaller genus of pterodactyls, making the whole event a bit anticlimactic.

Sam proceeded to give his typical lesson, though. "Pterodactyl is actually a term for a family of winged reptiles, also known as Pterosaurs. Some were cold blooded but others warm blooded."

"Did they evolve into birds?" asked Tommy.

Sam gave Tommy a look he'd given many people who'd asked the same question, the look you get from a special keeper of knowledge. "Nope. Oddly enough, birds evolved from terrestrial dinosaurs with feathers."

"I bet those were really ugly dinosaurs," Tommy said.

Sonata chuckled. Sam did not.

Tommy continued to ask questions: "What kind of sounds does it make?", "What does it eat?", "Isn't it getting lonely in there?"

Sam kept up with Tommy it for quite some time until finally he conceded, "I have some lab work to do this afternoon. Maybe we can meet back here tomorrow?"

"Of course," said Sonata before Tommy could object. "Can we explore the island this afternoon?"

Sam smiled. "Please do. There is a trail map in the main office. Don't forget bug spray and sunscreen."

The island was a lush rainforest. Hiking up one of the hills presented an opportunity to see plants and animals neither Tommy nor Sonata had ever seen. On the trail, Tommy told Sonata about a book he'd started writing.

"It's called *People Being Themselves Again*," said Tommy. "It's about what I see Culture Lab doing for people."

"That's a quite an undertaking for anyone, let alone for a ten-year-old," said Sonata.

"Someone has to do it." He spoke with the pensive tone of obligation, like a passenger helping a driver change a tire in the rain on a the side of a busy highway.

Sonata looked a bit confused. "Most kids your age say that about beating a video game, not writing a book."

"It's just so cool how all these really important, serious adults at Culture Lab started seeing things differently," Tommy said. "A few months ago they thought they were bigshot 'influencers' online. Now they don't have their social media following and they don't even seem to be missing it. They are going on adventures and having a lot more fun."

"That's exactly what I was hoping would happen with the project," replied Sonata. "Tell me more."

"Like the dollhouse Vic gave us. It sits in the lobby and adults sit by it and make up stories about family dramas that happen there."

Sonata stopped hiking, causing Tommy to stop, too. "Interesting. What do they do with the stories? Do they perform them for everyone?"

"No, sometimes they write out the stories with no intention of acting them out or really doing anything with them."

"That is wonderful," replied Sonata. "What kind of stories?"

"Oh well, it's a Chinese dollhouse, so some of them pretend to be members of a royal family in ancient China. Some people just pretend they are a modern family living there and come up with dramas like with a teenage boy throwing a party when he was told not to, or a mysterious creature living in the house, or whatever. It's entertaining to watch them. I've never seen adults behave like that before."

"Are you writing about that in your book?"

"Oh yeah, and all sorts of other stuff."

"Like what?" Sonata asked. Despite research predicting what could arise from Culture Lab, Sonata knew the whole thing was an experiment. Now she had Tommy, her least skilled, yet least biased researcher.

"Well," Tommy said, "you'll see all sorts of odd behavior, like people holding their open hand in front of them, looking at it as if they had a phone in it. That one is funny when they see me see them. Or when there was this broken gutter on the house, and they took it down and everyone worked together to fix it. It was like this pride thing for everyone. And I was like, 'Don't you all have houses? Is this the first time anyone's seen a broken gutter?'"

"Tommy, very few people live in houses. Most people are in condos these days. And no one tries to fix anything anymore. They just call someone."

"Sounds convenient," replied Tommy. "The tape they put on there will just weaken when it rains."

Sonata changed the conversation's direction. While she sought to embolden Tommy to pursue his potential, she also desired a greater attachment with him. "You see, Tommy, I picked you for this because few other kids would ask those types of questions. Few kids would be able to see these differences in people and write about them like you can."

"A lot of stuff changed for me when I lost my parents. It was like the whole world became my parents. I noticed more what adults around me were doing."

"You are so insightful, Tommy! I can't wait to read your book."

"Can I tell you an idea I had?"

"Of course," replied Sonata. They started hiking again.

"So this one is about pterodactyls. Each person gets one and they are like carrier pigeons, but they are bigger and can carry heavier stuff. What if you had a journal and you tied it to the pterodactyl's neck and the pterodactyl brought it to someone living far away? That person never learned your full name but got to learn all about your life. Then they tied their journal to their pterodactyl and you got to read about them. Or you could give the pterodactyl instructions for building a wood fort, and your friend from far away also gave him instructions. Then one day you could meet each other there."

"Wonderful ideas, Tommy. I'll have to ask Sam if pterodactyls could be domesticated."

"What does that mean?" asked Tommy.

"It means they will listen to people and follow instructions."

"Am I domesticated?" asked Tommy.

Sonata smiled. "Just enough, you don't want to be too domesticated, sweetheart." Sonata stopped for a second. *Did I just call him sweetheart? Maybe I really do want kids.*

At the top of the mountain, they had a view of Sam's complex and the beach below. Then Wyoming's face appeared to them in the water.

Tommy pointed his finger and raised his eyebrows. "That's him! That's the guy who appeared in the glass at the mall."

Sonata was speechless. Unlike Tommy, she'd never seen Wyoming before. "Is he nice?" she asked.

"Yeah, I guess. He is probably gonna talk more about the clock tower thing," said Tommy.

Sonata tilted her head forward, and a crease formed between her eyebrows. "What's that?"

"Oh, he said that if Culture Lab doesn't hurry up, the clock of culture would strike midnight and we'd all go back to cavemen." Tommy looked at the ground for a second. "The world would stink if we were all cavemen. Why do you think he's doing this?"

Wyoming's face remained silent in the ocean, as if waiting for the two to figure something out.

Sonata's initial disbelief wore off. "Did you tell me on the plane that before the mall thing happened, some people had dreams with him in them, and others didn't?"

"Some people said they never saw him in their dreams."

A clock on a brick pillar rose out of the ocean, high enough for Sonata and Tommy to read the time. Ten minutes to midnight.

Sonata's disbelief amped up again. "He said midnight was the reset, right?"

Tommy wiped his eyes to make sure he was seeing this correctly. "Yep, and it looks like we have ten minutes."

"Or ten days, or ten years," Sonata said. "Guess it just depends on how long a minute is in Wyoming's time."

*Maybe we were drugged on the airplane*, Sonata thought to herself. She didn't want to say this aloud to Tommy and cause fear. *But what would explain why Dad was picked first to see him, and all these people at Culture Lab, and now us?*

The face in the ocean dissipated into outward ripples and the clock tower lowered back into the water, with water quickly rushing in fill the void.

Sonata knew that no matter what was causing this, it had to be figured out. If the visions or hallucinations kept happening at Culture Lab, the participants would leave and her whole experiment would fail. If the clock really represented a deadline, she had to get moving.

"Are you okay running down the hill with me?" she asked Tommy? "I think we should be in a real hurry."

"I thought you'd never ask!"

They ran down the mountain together with such exhilaration Sonata felt her blood flowing through her arms and legs as she ran. She wiped the sweaty, matted hair away from her forehead. Tommy felt weak in his legs but he kept running. The whole thing was overwhelming, but being with Sonata made him feel like he'd be okay. She didn't try to explain anything away to him. She didn't minimize the situation or try to tell him it would all be fine, because she really didn't know if it would all be.

As soon as they got back, Sonata called her dad.

"Hello?"

"Dad, it's me. I have some big news."

"I thought you were on a business trip this week?"

"Yeah… Dad, I lied. Sorry. I am on a tropical island and we just saw…"

"You lied? You didn't want me there. That's fine, I guess."

"Dad, that's not… well, it's kind of true, but only because I wanted to hear more from Tommy about Culture Lab." Sonata knew she was still lying but considered it a white lie given the circumstances. "Dad, we saw Wyoming in the ocean and this clock tower rose out of the water and it read 11:50."

"Okayyy. Did Wyoming say anything this time?"

"Nope, just the outline of his face appeared in the water. Then the clock rose straight up. Tommy saw it, too."

"So does that mean ten minutes until the cultural armageddon?" asked Vic.

"Or ten years, or ten days. Who knows."

Vic smiled. "You had better get back home so we can make our dollhouse ad."

"Dad, what are talking about?

"That ad could be just the thing to jam up the gears in the clock."

"Okay, we'll fly home tonight."

"Bring some hotdogs or something on the plane, in case the pilot turns into a caveman before you do and you gotta do an emergency landing."

Sonata laughed. She needed a laugh. After hanging up, she and Tommy walked to the public kitchen at the compound on Pteradactyl Island and grabbed some hotdogs from Sam's fridge.

"So we can't eat these unless the pilot goes all ape shh on us?" asked Tommy.

Sonata looked at Tommy with adoring eyes. "I don't have buns or ketchup."

"That would be a problem."

In fourteen hours they were at the airport in Quelter, where they said their goodbyes.

"Tommy, Seth will be here any minute to pick you up."

"I don't want to go back to Culture Lab, I want to stay with you."

"I know. I'll see you soon. I need to make a Dandy Dollhouse ad with my dad to save the world."

Tommy smiled and let a puff of air out of his nose.

"For now. Can you do me a favor, Tommy, and stay hush hush about the whole clock tower thing? I don't want our participants getting hysterical."

"You mean you don't want them laughing a bunch?" replied Tommy.

"Ah… no, I mean losing their minds."

"Oh, double meaning, got it."

Sonata hugged Tommy, but this time got a real firm hug back, unlike before. Tommy put the side of his head into her stomach and hugged her lower back. In his hug she could sense his yearning for a mother.

# 23

# *Try Buying Something Boring*

Instead of knocking on the only functional door, the backdoor to her childhood home, Sonata walked in and set her keys on the entryway table. "Dad, I am home," she yelled.

She walked into the dusty living room, where Vic sat on a recliner watching TV. His head tilted to the side a bit, and his mouth was slightly open.

"Don't you know how to knock?" he asked.

"You would have preferred to get out of your recliner to come let me in?"

"Good point. Have you thought about the ad?"

"Yes, dad, and any ideas I come up with are painful and embarrassing."

Vic smiled. "Good. Well, I finished the script we started. Take a look at it and let me know what you think."

Sonata saw the script on the glass coffee table and sat on the old gray couch. The couch was actually gray and burgundy, with threads that crossed and alternated in color.

"Dad, when are you going to get rid of this ratty couch? I swear I remember Scout peeing on it many times as a kid."

"Just read the script and tell me what you think."

Sonata prepared herself to work with her father for the first time in over 30 years. She knew it meant a lot to him, because she sensed he felt inadequate as a father, despite her incredible success in life. This could be an opportunity to improve that. "Hmm… this is funny, Dad. So we're pretending I am a kid again and you are walking up the stairs, about to have a heart to heart with me about technology. Then you see me playing with a dollhouse and sit down and join. You know this commercial will make the board at Soradin, the biggest tech company on the planet, very unhappy."

"They can be unhappy all they want. Are you going to bow to them for the rest of your life?"

"Well, I was on a path to, until this demigod character came into our lives and made a clock tower rise out of the ocean. Now I'm re-evaluating my priorities. Plus, there is Tommy."

"Oh, what a nice boy. I bet you are thinking of adopting him."

"How did you know?"

"From time to time, I get a glimpse of what's in your heart. And I can tell that boy is in your heart."

"He sure is. But I am conflicted. I never met his parents. Maybe they'd want him to stay with his aunt."

"Maybe. There are a million things that could go right or wrong, whether he stays with her or you. So it comes back to how you both feel about it all now."

Sonata reflected. "Thanks Dad." She knew there was more to it than that but decided to give her father the satisfaction of having the answer.

Vic went back to script quickly, anyway. "Okay, therapy is over. Read the script and tell me what you want to change, omit, or add."

Sonata went up to her old childhood bed and edited the parody on her childhood. Her dad's writing was totally uninhibited, so she went with his flow. She grabbed the freshly sharpened pencil off the table and added a part where her dad would attempt to fix a floor leak. The plan was to poke a hole in the antique dollhouse floor and pour a thimble of water into it. Then Vic would soak up the water with a sock and put some glue in the hole. She would then say, "Dad, you're the best," and give him a big hug. Then they would hold hands and dance in a circle around the dollhouse. Cheesy and brilliant.

After she wrote in the edits and added parts, she gave it back to Vic to read through. It took him about five minutes before he returned to her.

"Good. When can we film this? And can we do the whole thing live?"

"Tomorrow at 5 p.m., and yes. I already called some higher ups at various networks and on various streaming platforms."

"So that leaves a whole day with just you, your mother, and I? Hot damn."

"Dad, no one has said hot damn for like 150 years. Do you read really old books or something?"

"As a matter of fact, since building dollhouses I started reading some classics from the 20th century. And it's just good to see you. Since you started with Soradin, I haven't seen you much."

That night the family had salmon and asparagus, with a raspberry tart for desert. After dinner, Gale shared her photos from Sandbush.

"Mom, these amazing."

"Thanks, sweetie. Thank god your dad had a heart-attack. I would have never left to Sandbush without all that chaos to stir things up."

"Hey, watch it," said Vic.

"I'll watch your heart monitor," quipped Gale.

As a therapist, Vic spent most of his emotional energy with his patients. So at home he was generally more closed off, and Gale and Sonata never quite knew what to do to make him happy. He smiled when Sonata earned a soccer trophy, or when Gale made him his favorite meal, but the joy didn't run deep. Now, in his later years, after his heart attack wake-up call, Vic could finally feel deep joy and connection to his family. But the quality of this new connection opened him up to some family jabs.

The next morning, the film crew arrived at the house at 9:30. As they set up cameras in Sonata's old room, Gale and Sonata brought out old boxes of toys to make it look just like it had when Sonata was nine. Vic had nothing else to do that morning, but wanted Sonata and Gale to have some time together, so he took a walk.

"Do you think kids today will even know what a doll is?" asked Sonata. "I mean, few people on the planet still own even one toy."

"Well, your dad says the ad is for kids and adults. Some of the older people will have seen these toys or heard about them," replied Gale.

Gale's blue room still had her twin bed in the corner, with a star constellation comforter and brass frame. Old, coarse teddy bears sat on the shelf above the bed and dolls sat in various small chairs in the corner of the room. In the middle of the room, on the old red, white, and blue rug, morning light illuminated Vic's grandmother's antique dollhouse. The white dollhouse radiated imagination and the chance for connection. It was accessible to anyone's heart.

On the first floor of the dollhouse were the kitchen and dining room. The office and master bedroom on the middle level put parents equidistant to family time downstairs and bedtime upstairs, where the kids' bedrooms were. The kitchen was kitschy, with a pink fridge, mini stove, mini table for dolls, and white wallpaper with tiny plastic blue flowers on it. The brown dining room table had four chairs, with one of the chairs holding an old wooden mini-baby chair in it. The living room had a mini deer head with antlers mounted on the wall. A red and black plaid design made the couch stand out in the room. One could consider the dollhouse a history lesson on gender roles in the $20^{th}$ century.

Most interestingly, Vic's grandmother specially decorated one of the two kids' rooms upstairs to represent what she wanted her childhood bedroom to look like. She drew planes all over waxy orange paper and carefully glued it to the walls with a glue stick. Grandma's little fairy figurine sat on a mini chair in the corner.

As Gale and Sonata were putting the final touches on the setting for the ad, Vic walked in. "Have you memorized your lines?" he asked.

Sonata gave Vic the exact same look she gave him in eighth grade when he suggested she conserve her popsicle sticks on her science-fair bridge.

"Okay, fine. I trust you got it."

"You guys are on for rehearsal at 11:00 a.m.," said the stage producer.

Sonata and Vic went downstairs and looked at old picture albums on the old gray and burgundy couch. They especially wanted to find a picture of Vic's grandmother, Kelly, as a kid with her dollhouse.

"That's her!" said Sonata. "She looks so happy!"

"Kelly in 1996," was written on the back of the picture. She was nine then. The dollhouse looked like it was from the earlier in the 20th century, maybe the 1950s. You could see she was creating a story about the characters in the dollhouse. The characters, all little figurines, were laid out on the floor in front of the house. It looked like a father, mother, son, daughter, a dog, and Kelly's little fairy figurine. On her bedroom wall hung a whiteboard with character names spread out and a web of lines between them. Above each line, the type of relationship and the quality of the relationship were noted. For instance, between Wendy and Tom the line said, "siblings, stopped talking to each other."

"Wow, that was 100 years ago," said Vic. "I remember grandma talking about the 1990s. She talked about the basic computers and cell phones that came out. She said everyone anticipated a gradual transition, with an unspoken hope for technology to integrate into the rhythm of cultural change, not to control it. Things were so different for her."

Now, computers were solely responsible for sustaining the human population and transmitting its culture. Artificial intelligence made adjustments to maximize food production and reduce waste from 40% to only 10%. AI could also predict where viruses would emerge, and new viruses were immediately reported online, allowing AI to often develop vaccines within days. AI robots also provided long-term care for the sick and elderly. Despite the consistency of care, people were dying sooner than expected, but without any objections to being cared for by robots. Had all this occurred a century prior, psychologists would have tried to understand why these people didn't object to AI care, but psychologists and therapists were a thing of the past. These positions were also taken by AI. Unless, of course, you lived in a resistor town like Vic and Gale.

AI controlled the spread of cultural information by directing people to new sources that fit their preferences. Most sources were short snapshots of a personal or cultural event, a moment in history, or a political decision. This is to say: people were no longer getting information in the form of stories beyond a few hundred words. On the level of the family, interest in genealogy and ancestry diminished, so people stopped telling elaborate stories, knowing they would no longer last beyond a generation. Perhaps most importantly, material objects were no longer circulating in society as the result of collective preferences for more stimulating computer experiences, and therefore were no longer a part of cultural transmission.

"You are on for your rehearsal in five minutes," said the stage producer.

"Alright, let's make this fun," said Vic.

"That's the first time you've ever said that," replied Sonata.

"Well, this is also the first time you and I have created something together."

"Okay, you got your lines memorized?" asked the director, who stood in the corner of the room next to the camera operator.

They nodded yes.

"Take your places!"

Vic walked down the stairs. Sonata sat on the floor next to her dollhouse.

"Action!"

The ad started with the camera focused on Sonata, thinking about which dolls she wanted in her play.

Vic knocked on the door. "Sweetie, can I come in?"

Sonata sat on her bedroom floor, playing with her dollhouse and trying to embody her nine-year-old self.

"Sure, Dad."

"Hey have you seen my… whatcha doin' there?"

Sonata held a small figure in her hand. "Oh, just playing with great-grandma's dollhouse. My character, David, is the dad and he's had a hard day at work. When he gets home, his daughter Chrissy is going to have some chili and cornbread for him. But I am thinking of melting the little plastic piece of cornbread just a little because it's Chrissy's first time and she messed up a little."

Vic walked into the room a bit and remained standing, looking down at Sonata. "Wow, you're making quite a scene. When did you get so creative?"

"Oh, I guess when I started playing with this dollhouse. For some reason it's more entertaining than my phone, but I really can't explain why."

"That's weird. Have you tried getting on social media or something? That could fix the problem."

"I tried that. I don't know, I just turned off the phone and I am thinking about this story I am writing."

Vic then kneeled down on one knee, just as choreographed in the script they wrote. "Well, tell me more about it," he prompted.

"Chrissy is not making dinner entirely because she loves her dad. She did something kinda bad."

"Oh yeah, like what?"

"Well, she knows the house is really old, and figured something needed to be repaired, but she couldn't find anything wrong, so she poked a hole through the floor. She got a pencil and poked it right through. Then she poured a little water through. You can see it still dripping."

"Chrissy did that, or *you* did that?"

"Well, technically, I did that."

"Oh sweetie. Before you do something like that again, can you ask me first?"

"Yeah. Okay. I'm sorry."

The eyes of everyone on set were lit up. This was the first time they'd seen Sonata Geraldine, the CEO of the world's biggest company, act like a kid. And this was all going to be all over the internet!

Vic sat down and looked at the hole. "Oh, this can be fixed in a jiffy."

He grabbed a kid's sock and some rubber cement, conveniently placed on Sonata's dresser. He soaked up the water and patched the hole with the glue.

Instead of saying, "Thanks Dad, you're the best," as the script dictated, Sonata said, "I wish you hadn't used my sock, Dad."

Vic didn't know what to do for a second. But he knew this was the chance to get closer to his daughter. "Sweetie, don't you think that sock is getting a little old?"

Sonata giggled at the joke, and an authentic smile exposed all her eye and forehead lines. She loved to see her dad just go with the flow for once. "Gee, thanks Dad, you're the best!"

The two stood up, held hands, and danced in circles around the dollhouse. They sang the classic tune "All 'round the brickyard" and replaced "brickyard" with "dollhouse." Then they let go and both looked at the camera.

"Hi, you probably all know me. I am Sonata Geraldine, CEO of Soradin, and this is my dad, Vic. Dad and I started this company called Dandy Dollhouses with the hope of awakening imagination and creativity in both kids and adults. These dollhouses can provide hours of fun by giving you a real-life, 3D place to write stories by yourself or with loved ones. Just looking at our dollhouses and these dolls generates tons of ideas because you are not bombarded with information and choices. In essence, these dollhouses are intended to be a bit boring to make you create. So go against the trend of over-stimulation and buy something boring!"

The director of the commercial didn't see this in script. As Sonata talked, he jotted a note on his phone and showed it the videographer:

"The board will be livid. I give her 24 hours."

Sonata knew the writing was on the wall, but she went on with the show. "Our dollhouses are custom, and when I say custom, I mean it. Tell 'em, Dad."

Vic smiled, knowing Sonata may soon leave corporate life, and that may mean more time with her. "Well," he said, "you can order dollhouses that represent cultures from the past. I know none of these cultures exist today, but you can remember them in your dollhouse. By remembering other cultures, you can change the world." Thinking about the clock tower, Vic wanted to say, "by remembering other cultures you can prevent a total cultural meltdown," but he held his tongue.

And finally, together, Vic and Sonata announced their big sales hook. "Try something new and order a Dandy Dollhouse today! If you put "Sonata and Dad" on your order form, your dollhouse will be 50% off!"

"Okay, cut! I wanted to stop you," said the director, "because Sonata, you and I may be out of work soon, but I loved it. You two are going to sell a lot of dollhouses."

"Just one take?" asked Vic.

"Oh yeah, I'm not going to get in the way of the right moment."

Sonata and Vic looked at each other and smiled. Sonata gave her father a hug, and when she pulled away she kept her hands on his shoulders. "I can't say why that was so fun, Dad, but thank you. For the past forty years, I've told the little girl inside me to go play while I chase success. Today I unlocked the room she was in."

Vic smiled while shaking his head a bit. "So you know you just stuffed your career into the trash, on top of already molding food?"

"Oh yeah, and then put some dog poop bags right on top of it."

"Will you be coming home?"

"I'm not sure, Dad, but I know we'll get more time together."

"Um, we're done here, so we're going to pack up," said the director awkwardly.

"Hey, Dad, it's getting stuffy in here, want to go for a walk?"

"Sure, let me get the dog."

Downstairs, Jasper laid in his dog bed. Although he just heard the word "walk," he wasn't interested. Their other dog, Rascal, a perky Yorkie, bolted up the stairs to greet his walkers. The hot day opened up seed pods of cottonwoods outside, and cotton-like material drifted through the sky, flowing with the wind.

**24**

# *Stories at Heart*

s Vic and Sonata walked down the street, they enjoyed shade from a row of large Sycamore trees. Sonata looked off to the hills east of town, now covered with golden bunchgrass. She focused on a mound of what looked like rock on the hill. *I don't remember it looking like that,* she thought to herself. But without her glasses she couldn't quite make it out.

She turned back to her father. "You're really okay with adoption? Last time I brought up even the idea of adoption, you cited all these studies where adopted kids developed some kind of addiction or mental illness later in life. You told me I wouldn't want to deal with that. You even had the gall to tell me I would not be able to solve my own difficulties in committing to a relationship by adopting a son or daughter."

Vic thought for a minute. "Most people get some mental health issue sometime in their lives. If people don't adopt kids who need homes, where else will they go?"

"So you're now going back on what you said?"

185

"I see you've formed quite a connection with Tommy and you experienced something pretty amazing together on that island."

Sonata looked back at the mound, which was changing. "Dad, what is that?"

Something burst through the mound on the hill to the east. Even without glasses, Sonata could see its man-made form.

Vic squinted to make it out. "Can you run in and grab the binoculars?" he asked Sonata. "They are on the table in my office."

Sonata ran off and Vic sat on the brown, dead grass strip between the sidewalk and the street. He sat in the shade of a Sycamore, with its branches swaying back and forth, allowing some sunlight to reach his face.

Inside, the stage producer stopped Sonata before she could make it to Vic's office. "Your ad has 12 million views and it's only been an hour," he said.

"Wonderful! Thank you so much. Now I hope you'll excuse me, I'm in a bit of a hurry."

Sonata ran back out with the binoculars. Vic had already stood back up.

"It's clearly a clock tower," she said. "Looks the same as the one we saw in the ocean."

"What does the time read?"

"Strange. Still 11:50."

Vic rubbed the white stubble on his chin like a detective. "Let's get a closer look."

To get to the clock tower they drove out on Highway 99 and took a left on the dirt road just past the peaches stand.

Then they drove up the road about five miles toward the hills. To their surprise, the town wasn't rushing over to see it. Most people were in their homes, on screens, with their AC cranked up full blast.

The clock tower stood about 30 feet out of the ground and leaned to the right. Its design was simple—a metal pillar with a clock mounted near the top. The clock face jutted from the tower, with the hands standing even further out.

"Do you remember if the second hand was frozen like that when you saw it in the ocean?" asked Vic.

"It was moving."

"Hmm… it was also moving in my dream. This clock is frozen."

"Maybe they just need to change the battery," quipped Sonata.

Vic followed along. "The battery, little did you know, is made of the unused idealism of today's apathetic population with their belly's full and their heart empty."

"So it freezing like this must mean people will get their idealism back!" replied Sonata.

Wyoming appeared, finally in a less surprising fashion, as himself in human form.

"Good idea, but no! Ha-ha-ha-ha! I don't normally do the ominous laughter thing, so I thought I'd try it out," he said.

"Why did the clock stop?"

"Because you did it! You got the world to pay attention to those dollhouses. Once they start playing with them, humans will believe in their own creativity again, and they will con-nect in new ways."

Wyoming wore a nicely fitted black t-shirt and blue jeans. He looked exactly the same as when Vic and Gale saw him in the local Quelter restaurant.

"So that's it, no going back to cavemen?" asked Vic.

"Not now. But you must understand something. Culture is a product of our creative ideas, and it's the foundation for our sense of purpose in life. Our aspirations, values, and fears are in relation to culture. We need this culture, this system, to work within, because it's a like the structure of a classroom, and we're all really just big kids."

"Where are you going with this?" asked Sonata.

"The world has become a culture of individuals. The benefit of this is the eradication of war and poverty because those are things we can all agree on. The downside is the responsibility for the creation of meaning is solely on the individual, not on their culture."

Now Sonata had a sense of where Wyoming was going with all this. "So what you're saying is our abundance in freedom, or lack of any obligations to our culture, puts us in tough situation where we must carry all the weight of traditions and values that used to come ready-made?"

"Exactly," replied Wyoming. "Now let me tie this all in to the dollhouse project."

Vic felt left out of the conversation. "Can I take a stab at it?" he asked.

"By all means, ha-ha-ha," replied Wyoming.

"You just gave him what he wanted, and you never do the ominous ha-ha-ha thing when you give someone something they want," said Sonata.

Wyoming nodded his head in recognition. "I've got to work on that."

"Anyway," said Vic, "kids will be the first to play with the dollhouses. The way we designed them allows kids to be creative while learning about cultures from the past. These dollhouses are a great way to see through the eyes of our ancestors. Since families stopped telling stories about their ancestors, kids have been craving them and not knowing it. These dollhouses meet that need, because kids will start making up their own stories, and without even knowing it, such stories will contain powerful themes their ancestors hoped to impart upon them."

"Exactly," said Wyoming. "In fact, the themes and values imparted in such stories are already in the subconscious minds of the children, and these dollhouses just activate them."

Sonata nodded in understanding. "And when adults see their kids writing plays and stories for the first time, they will naturally want to join in. It'll be like coming up for air from the technological ocean they are living in."

Wyoming looked at Sonata with admiration. "Nice words, coming from the CEO of the biggest tech company in the world. Speaking of coming up for air, I need to return home."

"Where is home?" asked Vic.

"It's where culture is created."

"Oookayy," said Vic and Sonata at the same time.

"This whole part of my speech may be a bit to chew on," replied Wyoming. "I'll make it quick because I really need to return home. In each person, there is a part of the mind uninhabited by the world's criticism and demands. I'll call the place the 'sweet spot' to make a point. It's a place where new ideas flash. The new ideas are connected to the needs or wants of a culture or individuals. Many creative ideas repeat in different people, but each person develops unique ideas all the time, whether they are conscious of it or not. All the sweet spots are connected to a generator of unlimited power. The generator lives in a different dimension, and I'm the mechanic. Now that humanity spends all its time consuming information and entertainment from computers, people have stopped drawing so much energy from the generator. As the mechanic, I figured the generator had a broken part but I couldn't find one. But I did read about the generator needing some constant draw of power of stay maintained. It's like a car that sits too long. Liquids start to leak and stuff starts to rust. After reading that, I came here."

Sonata looked fascinated and a little perplexed. "I'd say we learned something new today," she said.

With relaxed eyes and a half smile, Vic looked blissfully satisfied. "Thank you, Wyoming, for explaining this to us. And thank you for helping me get closer to my family."

"You bet, Vic. By the way, the ten million was a loan."

Vic rolled his eyes. "Oh no problem. So I'll just mail the check to 'Wyoming, Mechanic Shop, 5th Dimension Creativity Generator.'"

They both laughed, and then Wyoming was gone.

Sonata felt it necessary to draft a speech to relay Wyoming's message. She walked up to the clock tower and put her hand on the side.

"This clock tower will remain here for many years, even centuries, as a reminder to the people of Quelter to enjoy the little things in life, like antique dollhouses… That doesn't sound quite right. As a reminder to—"

"Stay connected to the people and stories that make them who they are?" chimed in Vic.

"Perfect. Thanks, Dad. You're the best."

"'You're the best?' Haven't heard that in… forty years?"

"Sorry. I've been scared to show appreciation. Sometimes you can be overbearing, and maybe I thought showing appreciation could feed that controlling side of you."

"Sorry about that, sweetie. I've never realized how overbearing I was until this all happened. Part of it is just not knowing how to really love someone. Part of it is thinking I know best because people paid me to tell them what's best for them, even though we would pretend I am just a good listener with good questions."

"Finally, a therapist comes out with it!" Sonata joked.

"I also enjoy poking at your stubbornness a bit," admitted Vic, "even if your stubbornness led to your success."

There was a pause between the two.

"Give any more thought to moving home?" asked Vic.

"As much as I would want to, a 47-year-old billionaire living at home with her parents is kind of a funny idea, right?"

"It's as funny as you make it."

"Dad, I promise to be closer to you from now on, but I can't live at home. Plus, you and mom are moving to the cabin in Sandbush, right?"

"Yeah, probably. Think I'll hire someone to watch over Dandy Dollhouses. What a stupid name. Why did I come up with that name?"

"It's a great name. Has a timeless feel."

On the way to the airport, to send Sonata back to Sora-din to empty her office, she opened Vic's glove box in his old 2050 truck. She pulled out a black leather-bound book with no writing on the cover or spine. "What's this?" she asked.

"It's my journal. Open it up."

"Oh, Dad, this is personal…"

"No, not really. I just started journaling so there isn't much in there yet. I suggested it to my clients but never really did it myself."

Sonata opened the journal and found a dollhouse sketch on the first page. On the second page, Vic sketched Sonata and Gale in t-shirts and shorts. *That was the day we walked him into the surgery*, she thought. On the third page was a large sketch of a heart with four arteries, each an inch wide. At the end of each artery, Vic wrote four areas of focus for him: "Sonata, Gale, Purpose, and Change." Each artery looked to be a little blocked, and Vic wrote some notes on how to break up the blockage. For Sonata, he wrote, "create something together." For Gale, he wrote, "let her fly." For "purpose" he wrote, "dollhouses," and for "change" he wrote, "let people in."

*Let people in?* Sonata wondered.

Vic glanced at the page and noticed Sonata's finger on "change."

"Let you and Gale in. Let my close friends in. Stop being so closed off and in control all the time," he clarified.

"The mechanic finally fixes his own car!" Sonata joked, referring to the stereotype of mechanics having a bro-ken-down car at home.

Their last few months together were full of laughter, understanding, and timelessness. Despite a successful heart surgery and burst of energy from his personal transformation, Vic passed away later that year. A sudden pancreatic cancer hit him, and while in pain for the last two weeks of his life, he was free of fear.

# 25

# *A Peek Through Tommy's Eyes*

After returning from Pterodactyl Island last night, I've been thinking more about whether Sonata will adopt me than Wyoming's face out in the ocean. She never brought it up, but I bet she is thinking about it. The way she smiled at me, and asked me all these questions; no one's ever asked me so many questions about myself.

I just wish I could have my parents back. I wish I didn't have to make such big decisions. I already said yes to Culture Lab, which means missing out on a normal kid life. Adults are really interesting and really boring at the same time. I could be in class passing notes, or with friends biking around some dangerous construction site, or playing basketball and failing miserably but having fun. Sometimes I wonder what Mom and Dad would want for me if they were alive to tell me. It's hard to imagine. How would I look back on this at twenty years old? Oh man, twenty seems so old! If I am hanging out with all these people who are in 30s and 40s now, by then I'll be hanging around people in their 40s and 50s. That's just too old.

"Knock, knock. Rise and shine, sunshine." Cecelia knocked on my door every morning with the same amount of gusto.

"Be right there, gotta brush my teeth," I answered with fake excitement.

Honestly, Cecelia's gusto was impressive. Wyoming cast a dark cloud on Culture Lab, but Cecelia stayed positive and never lost her optimism.

As I brushed my teeth, I looked in the mirror at my hair, which was now over my ears and almost in my eyes. I wondered what short, like really short, hair would look like. When I was all ready to go, I stepped out the door and Cecelia was right there.

"How did you sleep?" she asked on our way to breakfast.

"Surprisingly well after yesterday."

"Did he, it, really make the outline of a face in the water?" she asked.

"Yep. But if I had his powers, I'd make a spiral or flame shape, something more interesting."

"Tommy, we missed you."

"Do you miss me, or my envied sense of humor?"

"It is true, Tommy. Somewhere down the line, most of us adults misplaced our humor like a set of keys."

When Cecelia said that, I had to remind her, "How many times do I have to tell you all the keep your house key in the same place on the entry table in your room!"

"Six billion, eighty million, one hundred and thirty-six thousand and three, to be exact."

"Ah jeez. I give up. I'm just going to buy super powerful magnets and hold them outside of your door. Then your keys and watches, and perhaps even nails holding up art in your room, will fly to the door and stick there, and *then* you'll never lose your keys." I'd come to see humor made me likeable to adults, and being likeable meant being loveable. And being loveable meant I'd be safe here. I knew that's why I told jokes. But I also just liked telling jokes.

They served breakfast out on the back patio and back lawn because it was finally warm enough outside. Ten people had left Culture Lab, so there were less round tables and more space to walk around. Walking to get my food from the long tables at the corner of the lawn was the most annoying thing here. I had to endure all the looks people gave me, looks that said, "Wow he's such a brave kid, coming out here after losing his parents," or "His aunt really took him out of school for this?" Either way, they sent judgement missiles with their eyes and I couldn't figure out how to send a counter-attack.

Once I made it to the breakfast table, everything got easier. Today I sat by Cecilia and enjoyed my pancakes with blueberry sauce and sausages. They actually have lots of food choices here, which is nice.

In the middle of breakfast, Sonata started her speech on the stage they built. She said that the culture clock was stopped, for now. No threat of suddenly forgetting how to give commands to a self-driving car or AI housecleaner, even though the first thing was a really big deal and the second not so much. No masses of people hoarding food at grocery stores. We could all go back to our lives of comfort and ease.

She looked so calm up there, speaking to the group. Maybe she'd make a cool mom after all. Having tons of money is a bonus. As she spoke, I reminisced about my mother. I miss her combing my hair, tucking me in, and telling me stories about the family before bed. I'd tell my friends at school about her stories and they were amazed because none of their parents told them stories. No wonder Mom said storytelling was a dying art.

One story she told me was about a shooting star she'd wished upon. She said she wished to feel like everything in life made perfect sense, just for one day. That it all added up to something, and that we could rest in knowing that. And her wish came true. The following day, she didn't complain about her job, her boss, or even about the school system that replaced teachers with AI "learning buddies." She said she told me this story, and only me, because no one else would believe a shooting star wish could actually come true.

Mom told me that story shortly before she and dad went missing. After they went missing, I spent all my time on the computer researching what could have happened to them. It was just so unlikely. No one these days was desperate for money, so they wouldn't have been held ransom.

Eventually I gave up and started to think they just hated their jobs, their life, and even me, and they'd run from it all. But my aunt assured me every night before bed that they would never do that. She promised me and I believed her. That's when things started to get better. I started to accept it all, and try to move on with my life.

Cecelia interrupted my reverie. "Tommy, you've only taken one bite of your food, and it's normally gone by now. Is everything okay?"

"I think I want to leave Culture Lab and go back to school next fall." The words came tumbling out of my mouth like rocks down a hill.

"Wow, okay, what made you decide on that?"

"I've been thinking about my life, and I can't run from it just because my parents are gone. I don't want to miss out on being a kid.

"Tommy, that's a very mature thing for you to say."

"Thanks. You know, being around sixth graders will take some getting used to at first, but I'll find my people. I've got to get in with the bullies first. Say the right things to keep them from smelling my fear, and then shift to the nerdy kids in a way that seems like I am pitying them, even though I'd prefer to hang out with them."

Cecelia looked interested. "Don't you think the nerdy kids will get mad?"

"Yeah, but then I'll tell 'em my plan."

After Sonata finished her speech, I decided to tell her, too. She was pouring an iced tea at the table in the corner of the backyard when I walked up to her.

"Hey Sonata, I gotta tell ya something."

"Sure Tommy, I am all ears." She put her too-full cup down slowly and turned to me.

"Well, I think I want to leave Culture Lab and go back to school."

Sonata picked her cup back up and took a sip off the top. "Had enough of us boring adults?" she asked.

"Oh, you are all amazing and I love it here. I just gotta go try to be a normal kid for a while."

"Okay Tommy, well something's been on my mind, too."

*Oh boy*, I thought. *Either she wants to talk adoption or she found out how I added a mechanical arm in the Culture Lab soda machine to shake them before delivery.*

"Tommy, I think your Aunt Tanya is wonderful, and she sure does love you, but I've come to love you as well, and… I would be happy to have you come live with me."

At this point I needed a glass of my own ice tea, so I poured one while Sonata awkwardly waited for my response.

"Are you saying you want to adopt me?"

"Yes, that's what I am saying."

"Um, let me think about it. I kind of have mixed emotions. On one hand, my aunt is sweet and doesn't have a lot of money, and on the other, you are sweet and have a lot of money. Guess when I put it that way, it isn't such a hard choice."

Sonata laughed, and a tear welled in her eye.

I was joking, because I don't just care about money, but the whole thing was awkward and telling jokes was the way I knew how to get out of the mucky awkwardness.

"Think about it, Tommy." She hugged me and walked away. Just after making a huge decision to go back to school, I got slapped with another decision about where to live. "I'm only eleven," I told myself. "Wait, I'm eleven!" My birthday was a week earlier, but with everything going on, I totally forgot about it. Back at the breakfast table I told everyone about my birthday, and that night they made me a cake and the whole community sang happy birthday to me. Balean even scrambled to buy me some planes to paint and new clothes.

After dinner and the birthday party, I went to bed and laid awake thinking about Sonata's offer. I couldn't think of a reason to say no.

# 26

## *Back to School*

By August, I went from living in a cramped house with too many people to living in a mansion with just Sonata. She didn't even have to ask if I wanted her to leave her little apartment and go big. She knew a small apartment wasn't going to cut it for me. I mean, I am not like just about money and stuff, but it's nice to have.

The house came fully stocked with a soda machine, snack machine, model airplane room, basketball court, and go-cart track. It even had a cool garden with tons of strange plants, a coy pond, and a place to sit. We called it the "Special Intelligence Headquarters" because it was a place where we could both think.

Sonata thought about what she wanted to do for all the people who were sad and lonely in the world. She told me human brains had a special space for traditions, rituals, and spirituality, and all the time we spent in front of screens drowned out the sound from that compartment. She wondered how to quiet the world for people so they could hear from the part of them that facilitated meaning in life.

At the Special Intelligence Headquarters I thought about very different things than Sonata. I thought about teaching a mouse house to operate a small airplane, like model planes but with an engine. I would, of course, have a controller to take over in case the mouse forgot what to do. Each time the mouse performed a sequence of tasks, like start engine, push throttle, etc., it would get a reward by way of an electrical signal to the brain.

Soon I'd have to start thinking about school. I would step into my first classroom in a long time on September 4th. In fact, I hadn't been in school since fourth grade and kids changed a lot between fourth grade and sixth grade. Sonata put me in a private school with mostly real teachers instead of AI buddies, which is a good idea in theory, but one with more potential for public embarrassment.

On the day before school, I sat in the flower garden and wrote in my journal about how I wanted things to go. I thought about how I wanted to make real, lasting friendships and not just be part of a herd. But I was worried most kids my age didn't ever think like that.

At first I wondered if I'd say something in class that was weird or stupid or even too smart. Ya know, that one adverse comment could destroy any chance of anyone wanting to be my friend. Then the deeper issue, the one of not having my real parents anymore, set in. How could I figure out how to avoid talking about it?

As I journaled and listened to the birds chirping, Sonata walked over.

"Hey Tommy, can I sit with ya?"

"Sure, Sonata." We were both clear that there was no expectation I'd call her mom. She sat near me on the bench looking out over a oval flower garden with pathways going around it.

"I am going to guess that you are thinking about tomorrow," she said.

"Oh yeah, I'm nervous."

"I'm not going to tell you not to be. You have reasons to be nervous."

"Can't we just get an AI buddy here to teach me?" I asked. "I promise not to reprogram it to jump off a bridge."

"Ha, you know we'd just buy another if you did. But that's not the point. You made this decision, Tommy, you should stick to it. Besides, making friends your age is good for you. It could help you let go of the weight you carry about your parents and trying to understand their disappearance."

"There is nothing that will lift that weight."

Sonata looked out at the tulips and carnations. "Maybe not, but do you want to look back on these years and see a very smart but very lonely child painting planes and running experiments, spending all his time talking about serious stuff with adults like me? Or a kid who got to be a kid and live a kind of normal life?"

"What do you know about a normal life? You were raised in Quelter, a resistor town trapped in a different time. Then you went on to get all these degrees and start all these companies and become super successful. I wouldn't say that's very normal."

Sonata sighed, like someone on a hike who got to what they thought was the top, only to look up at yet another steep climb. "You are a tough cookie," she said.

"Tough cookie?"

"My dad called me that because I was so stubborn."

"It's a weird saying because you eat cookies, and you don't try to eat stubborn people," I said. We both needed a laugh. "I'll *try* to see your point and give school a try, but I'll need to talk to you about it every day because it's scary."

"Of course, Tommy. I'll be here. We can talk whenever you want." She looked at her watch. "Well, I should run, I have a… date."

"A date? I thought you didn't date." I feared once Sonata found a guy she wouldn't be around as much, but I couldn't tell *her* that.

"I didn't date for a long time, but I've started to see how it could be good for me, and for you, too. I don't want to be a helicopter parent, spending every second hovering above your life."

"Fair enough," I said. I gave her a quick hug, which sometimes meant more than a long hug.

That afternoon, I grabbed my skateboard and went to the local skatepark. It had been two years for me, but I needed to put myself out there. Talking to other kids was even scarier than trying some old tricks.

The next morning, Sonata drove me to Welingster Academy. She kissed me on the forehead and said I'd do great. On the steps up to the school, I noticed a kid in blue jeans with white faded areas, a leather backpack with a string-synch instead of a zipper opening, and brown, combed back hair. Maybe he could tell I was looking at him, and he stopped and turned back to me.

"Hey I am Alex," he said. He put out his hand to shake mine.

"Tommy," I said. I shook his hand but felt awkward about it. "I thought the name Alex went out of style a long time ago."

"My parents wanted to give me a classic name, like yours."

"Right, classic. You can be Alexander the Great and I can be Tommy, the… "

"Train?" Alex finished my sentence.

"Exactly, I can use my train whistle to send out a bully warning so you can prepare for battle while I choo choo away."

We walked and talked on our way to class. Our first class was coding, which seemed stupid to me because AI could do all the coding the world needed. In fact, the school would set us all up to become coders, doing tasks we weren't needed for. It seemed no one asked questions though, because it beat unemployment. In another class I learned about the unemployment and homelessness of the 21st century. I always wondered how they got people on the street to get off drugs and take coding jobs. They must have brainwashed them somehow.

In history we talked about the world's leap out of poverty. When I asked why people trusted AI to manage economies, remote education, and development of poorer countries, my teacher looked surprised. After a pause he said, "Great question, Tommy. My guess is that people finally accepted they weren't smart enough to ever raise the whole world out of poverty."

My favorite part of the day was lunch. Alex and I sat outside in the courtyard, at a table under this cool magnolia tree with flowers blooming. We talked about all sorts of stuff. His parents were gone, too, but not missing. They worked in rare jobs that kept them traveling most of the year. When I asked Alex what his parents specifically did for work, he said, "I don't really know." He was raised by a nanny, and he was an only child like me. Despite some mean looks, and a few put-downs about my immediate teachers' pet status, the first day went well because of Alex being there.

The second day, however, went down a dark alley. Sost hadn't shown up the first day, but did show up on the second, and he arrived with a bang. Literally. Well, it was more of a pop, or crack.

The history teacher was just about to start his lesson, and *crack*, a metal ruler slapped the desk. Sost held the ruler, smiling. "You must be Sost," said the teacher. "Bring me the ruler." Sost walked up to the front of the class with the ruler. On his way, he slapped me in the arm with it.

"Office, now!" said the teacher.

Sost threw the ruler against the wall and walked out.

"I'm sorry, Tommy, are you okay?" he asked.

"Yeah, fine. I think a little welt is forming, but I'll be fine."

"If you need to see the nurse, let me know."

"What's with him?" asked Alex.

The teacher sighed and looked around the room. I could tell he was thinking of some pre-packaged response. "His parents came from a resistor town and he was raised without much technology. My guess is he felt insecure about that when we opened our laptops today."

After half an hour, they called me into the principal's office to give Sost an opportunity to apologize.

The office walls were covered with digital screen tiles of different sizes. It looked like you could actually resize them.

One tile showed data on student learning, another showed the principal's family, and another had the principal's calendar. I couldn't help myself. I tried to touch one, and it beeped at me.

"It only responds to my fingerprints," said the principal.

"Cool."

Sost sat in the chair across the principal's desk with his head hanging down.

"Come have a seat, Tommy, Sost has something to say to you."

"Sorry," he said, with as much authenticity as he could muster in front of the principal.

"All good," I said. "Alex and I eat lunch by the trees with the big white flower petals in the courtyard. Wanna come hang with us today?"

Sost looked up at me. "Really?" he asked.

"Yep."

That day, Sost joined us. Now, as a group of three, we were more bully-proof. And by the end of the week, I had invited both Alex and Sost over to my new mansion.

**27**

# *Burdened Choices*

Instead of spending his middle school years adventuring, journaling, and trying to summon Wyoming back at Culture Lab, Tommy spent his time in school and with his friends. He quit racing to become an adult, but after a few years of things feeling normal, certain events disrupted his pursuit of a semi-normal childhood. In the summer after Tommy's eighth grade year, Alex became obsessed with virtual reality and spent more and more time at home on his headset. Sost's dad died of a form of cancer AI had yet to cure, causing Sost to spend more time at home and withdraw from social situations. And worst of all, Sonata met someone Tommy didn't think was quite right for her.

He tried to adjust to the new situation at home, and in high school without his friends. But a loneliness set in, one he tried to transcend with fantasies of being a great world leader. He imagined giving grand speeches and waking people up to their situation. He began to believe humanity had surrendered to mediocrity. Most people lived and worked in single-room condos, coded all day, and received entertainment

207

from screens in the evening. While the world's loneliness was indeed a problem, he made it his problem, perhaps because a cause could be more dependable and loyal than a person.

Instead of looking to drugs to numb out his feelings, Tommy began to reconsider the merits of living an alternative life at Culture Lab. Maybe living among such intelligent, influential people would be just thing to catapult Tommy into his dream of leadership.

So, halfway through freshmen year, at barely 15 years old, Tommy decided to return to Culture Lab. He had to talk to Sonata first, as he didn't want to hurt her. One day he approached her in the garden, the designated place for their more serious talks. She sat on her bench near a bird bath with a pensive look on her face.

"I'm leaving and going back to Culture Lab," he said.

"Why is that?"

"I think it's a chance for me to grow into a leader."

"Tommy, I see how it could be hard for you, not quite being grown up yet having the choice to live wherever and with whoever you want to. Look, I know I've been away with Darrel more often, and I know you're more disconnected from your best friends in middle school. But I wish you'd hang in there."

"I gave it a try, the whole normal kid thing, and I just ended up being disappointed." Tears welled in Tommy's eyes.

Sonata didn't know what to say to make it right, so she just put her arm around him. "As your legal guardian, I could technically stop you, but I won't. Go to Culture Lab and follow your dreams. But just know that you could get hurt there, too. There is no dream to protect you from getting hurt, Tommy."

Tommy expected his return to Culture Lab to be as comfortable as his initial arrival at 11, but some things had changed. First, since Sonata stepped down from Soradin, the company quit sponsoring the project. Baelen took over, and the project ran solely on donations. This gave Baelen more creative freedom, with which he tried all sorts of weird ideas, including requiring Tommy to sign an oath to create one new tradition idea a week. Not just a tradition for the people at Culture Lab, but one that could spread once the participants were "released back into the wild," of society.

To spite Baelen, Tommy thought of weird things like sucking a few spaghetti noodles through a straw at the beginning of a spaghetti dinner. This was supposed to symbolize the difficult journey of change throughout one's life. He told Baelen they could really perform this tradition at any dinner with noodles. While having fun with it all, Tommy also seriously considered what type of impact this project, now years beyond its anticipated timeline, would have on society.

Arush and Cecelia had stuck with the program and treated Tommy like a son. They showed him the plays they wrote for the dolls and dollhouse Vic donated, the new traditions they embraced, and pictures of their wedding. "I knew you two would get married," Tommy had said when he saw the rings. The community worked together to home-school Tommy, who had a resident status at Culture Lab and decided to embrace a community of adults as his teachers, guardians, and friends.

# 28

# *Culture Templates*

When Tommy turned 25, Baelen stepped down as Director of Culture Lab and voted Tommy in as the new director, fulfilling his dream of leadership.

After a few months in the position, Tommy wrote a speech to the community to celebrate its advancements. He gave the speech during breakfast, as morning was the most stimulating part of the day at Culture Lab.

**Speech by Tommy Geraldine, 2127**

"Years ago, when Sonata adopted me, she knew how much I loved my parents and understood they could never be replaced. She figured such tragedy would make coping with life's challenges difficult for me, but she also hoped it would give me a richer view of life's meaning. She figured it could open me up to the types of adventures humanity desperately needed. Some events in life are so troubling and confusing, they freeze us in fear, shame, doubt, and resentment. As a kid, I didn't have the tools to look deeply at these forces, but I was willing to say yes to unusual adventures because my parents' disappearance left me with early inner wisdom about the preciousness of life.

So here I was, this eleven-year-old boy, taking trips around the world, and being raised by a bunch of strangers, and none of them fully knew the point of all this. They were told they were part of an experiment to grow new cultures. They were the milk, and our adventures were the lactic acid. Sonata herself didn't believe she could really grow new cultures. She hoped to just see how people could change after being removed from personal devices for a few years. She hoped people would dig deep inside and reclaim their need to feel part of a tribe. But marketing the whole thing as a "culture lab" appealed to the ego.

Despite her doubts, I am proud to say Culture Lab has created three new culture templates with distinct languages, beliefs, customs, toys, and tools. Fortunately, participants wanted to stay longer than three years to see this through. Well, if I am being honest, I think we all wanted to see Wyoming come back and make some strange balloon shape out of Soradin headquarters.

Developing new languages was a big undertaking. Some years ago, I started designing a device to garble up one's words, and proposed participants wear the device a few hours a day for one year. The theory was that they would alter their speech to make English come out of the device, and after taking the device off, they would have a new language. Then the linguist in the group got to work on the grammar of it all.

Beliefs were tricky, too. Scientific reasoning and the habit of observing and analyzing constantly filled up the cognitive domain of belief in one's psyche. To create room, we cut off participants from academic books and papers, and obviously from the media. We brought scientific kits in and encouraged experimentation and visceral experience. It wasn't that academic sources were wrong, it was more about engaging with knowledge in a new way and creating space for wonder.

Thirteen years ago, something happened to make Wyoming disappear. Sonata told me he went away not because the world woke up from its apathy, but because she and her dad reunited while making their advertisement for Dandy Dollhouses. We still have one of the first models in the common area. Anyway, my point is, this demigod who visited us in our dreams, who pulled a glass ceiling up into a dome and appeared in it, and who made us afraid of reverting back to cavemen, decided to just go away because a daughter and father reunited. This character is still out there, and I believe he could restart the culture clock at any time. So I say we follow through with what Sonata started. I think it's time we take all these ideas into the world.

Tommy received a standing ovation. During the clapping, Tommy felt mixed emotions. He felt well-deserved praise and credibility, and he felt some shame about taking this path instead of a more conventional one. He had a flashback of those middle school years with his close friends. He remembered playing football on jetpacks with them. He thought of Sonata. He remembered wondering how a billionaire could be a real person. He remembered sensing her fear of starting a family, as someone who'd just lost his. He now shared that same fear and wondered if it would ever leave him.

After taking some questions from the crowd and joining them for dinner, Tommy went back to his room, and back to his deep inner conflictions.

Just then Sonata called.

"What's up, Mom?" asked Tommy.

"Oh just wondering how the speech went."

"Great. I told them we were going out into the world."

"Wow, how did they respond?"

"With applause. I was surprised, thinking they just wanted to stay in this utopia."

Tommy split the 50 people in Culture Lab into three groups of 16-18 people each, each group representing a "Culture Template."

"Keep in mind," Sonata warned, "participants were originally meant to be released in Quelter, to cushion their culture shock. Are you planning to do that or release them somewhere else?"

"Somewhere else. I think they may try to create a mini-utopia in Quelter and defeat the whole purpose."

"Okay, how about you release them in three different cities?" proposed Sonata.

Tommy sighed. "I worry that in a big city, it won't take long for them to split up and forget their culture entirely."

"You don't know that. Some of these people have been here for years. We really can't say what they will do. Plus, a big city has the potential to spread a new culture more quickly."

"What if the culture shock it too much for them and they all come back?"

"Tell them to try and stay out for a year. Tell them about the importance of their mission. Tell them… tell them they possess something buried in the hearts of billions of people. Not only a feeling of belonging, but a feeling of continuity to the past and the future, because that's what living within a culture is all about."

"The way you said it sounds much more inspiring than how I can say it."

Sonata blushed, and although they were on the phone, Tommy could sense it. "Okay, Tommy, just take a picture of me, print it on a large paper, cut out my head, and glue it to mask you'll wear. Say I am wearing my mother's confidence. Then they'll think you're nuts and be ready to get out there."

Tommy laughed. "It's worth a shot."

Tommy called together all the members of Culture Lab that night to make a plan for re-entering the world. For most participants, it had been 15 years. The three groups worked in different culture areas.

Group A had worked in the gardens. Over the past few months, they'd created two new drugs by mixing compounds from plants. One drug reversed Alzheimer's and the other halted the spread of cancer cells. They decided they were going to leave their medicines at Culture Lab, and instead teach people about plants. They would show people a variety of medicinal plants and give them some guidelines for combining compounds and testing them. This way people could independently develop medicines instead of spending their hard earned money on pharmaceuticals. The group conferenced on how to build trust with people from the dominant culture.

Group B quietly walked around the grounds most days, fasting and meditating. They chose a more radical intervention. They decided to create a campaign for their city to be quiet for a day. The quiet included no talking and no electronic devices. In that space, the group theorized, unnoticed aspects of daily life would get noticed and broken parts of the city's social machinery would get repaired. In a classroom, students are often more receptive to the emotions of other students than the teacher is. Their relationship with the outer world has yet to concentrate in the thinking mind. Their intuition, feelings, and sensations still dominate. A quiet city creates an opportunity to feel more, to see how others feel, and to catch those chances to be more in touch with people who've been on the periphery.

Group C created a play with elements of Greek tragedy and tribal cosmology. Group C took the least culturally invasive approach by simply starting acting classes in their city. It had been fifty years since acting classes were offered, and this group believed classes could restore a joy in relating with others without anything to lose or gain.

The next morning, Tommy sat on the back patio, wondering how this would all work out. It was winter in Quelter. A morning dove sat calmly in an alder tree, holding space for Tommy's reflection.

*What if someone is arrested for some bogus cause? What if the culture shock is traumatic? What if no one believes these groups jumped on a new track, separate from the dominant culture of the world?*

He wondered about these things, and then began to wonder more deeply: *I wonder what Mom and Dad would have thought of Culture Lab.*

Tommy sat in his Adirondack chair and scratched the sparse stubble on his face. His hair stayed a light brown, drawing attention to his blue-green eyes. He was handsome, and yet terrified of women, and knew it had to do with losing his parents. Yet a part of him found peace around the issue. After all, he could end up in the history books as the one who renewed the human spirit during the global apathy epidemic. As he sat in this chair, reflecting, Vic came to him in the form of a letter that had blown into the yard. Tommy stood up, grabbed the piece of paper, and sat down to read it.

Dear Tommy,

I miss you, buddy! Say, do you have my glasses? Sonata may have donated them when I passed, but those specs had real silver frames. If you find them, put them on your dresser and I will snatch them in the middle of the night.

The afterlife is just awesome. First off, I got a tour of space where all the scientific mysteries of the universe were revealed to me. Yes, the Big Bang is true, and just for your information, "Ode to Joy" sounded throughout all of space while it happened. I got to explore it all for myself. Oh, and the creator of the universe threw a spiritual party the other day. Just imagine a dance hall light years across, with spinning galaxies instead of chandeliers or disco balls.

You've taken on quite some responsibility. I felt that way about dedicating the last years of my life to building dollhouses, but I made a decision and stuck to it. As you release these people into "the wild," be open-minded with your expectations.

There is nothing they can do to tarnish your name or your vision. Just have fun with it.

And take care of Sonata in her older years! Her life accomplishments are like an extra gravitational force, aging her.

Love, Vic

P.S. The clock tower will start ticking again unless you release your cultures into the world.

The "p.s." should just mean "one more thing," not "one extremely scary thing, sorry."

Tommy folded up the letter, went to his room, and put it in his childhood toy chest. This would have really freaked him out had he not had those encounters with Wyoming as a kid.

The next morning, Tommy had a few more things to tell participants based on the letter. He figured they could make a cultural impact with the pressure off, only if it came from a sincere place.

"I hope you are all excited to see the world out there. When you all arrive, you can expect an immediate submersion into the dominant culture's technology. It will feel like jumping into a maze with a timer. Resist the temptation to share your cultural ideals through the internet. They will just become ripples in collective thought. The only way to reach people is by talking with them in person. In fact, if that's all you do, without transmitting any new culture, then you can say you've succeeded.

"What if we are convinced the way everyone else does things is better?" asked a member of group A.

A somber look came over Tommy's face. "Then you've failed your mission."

Everyone paused.

Tommy smiled. "Just kidding! If you completely conform to the dominant culture over the course of a year, then enjoy your new life! For those who want to come back, you know where to find me."

That afternoon, everyone departed on their way into the unknown.

# 29

# *Into the Cultural Void*

Zaft, a member of culture group C, was one of the first members of Culture Lab. He was there when Tommy showed up, and he was there to see Wyoming create a glass dome in the old mall. Before coming to Culture Lab, Zaft tried being an actor, and then a writer.

He tried acting in advertisements that still wanted human actors instead of digital representations. After spending a decade getting really good at selling things he didn't care about, Zaft started writing books and giving popular online talks on self-actualization. But even that burned him out. At a point of utter despair and lack of direction, Zaft received an offer to come to Culture Lab.

Now, after living at Culture Lab for over 15 years, he was well into his 50s. Although his hair had turned gray, it was still wavy, and the olive skin on his face was still smooth and unblemished. He wore a warm tan button-up shirt and stretchable cargo pants practically every day. Like most of the residents, Zaft didn't want to leave Culture Lab, but Tommy said it would be good for him. "Just leap, and trust you can swim," Tommy had told him.

On the plane out of Quelter, he started to recollect Soradin commercials he'd acted for before getting to Culture Lab. He remembered one ad in particular.

"Feel like you have everything you want, but life is still empty? Tired of longing for more purpose in life? Try Soradin's new Revolution Simulator. This VR game puts you at the forefront of a revolution to overthrow a tyrannical government. Or you could try our Great Sacrifice game. In this near reality game where you categorize all of your belongings and then pretend to throw them away as part of a spiritual mission. So why wait? Open the Soradin app, and have your game downloaded in less than a minute!"

"Glad I left that place," Zaft said aloud.

"What place?" asked the woman next to him.

"Oh, sorry, did I say that aloud?"

"Yes… you said more than that. I think I'd like to try the Great Sacrifice Game. Or better yet, I could actually just give away all my stuff."

"The game is not nearly as painful as actually giving it all away," replied Zaft.

"Oh yeah?"

"Yeah, about 15 years ago I moved to this place called Culture Lab and gave away 95% of my stuff. The car was the most difficult to part with. Handled great, all leather seats, and my own AI friend to talk with in the car."

"So are you going to Derise on a business trip?" asked the woman.

"You could say that. My business is to rejuvenate the human spirit by recruiting people to take my acting class. Man, saying that sounds ridiculous."

"Acting class? In-person classes haven't existed for a century. Why do you think people would want to come to your group class when they can take any class they want in their living room?"

"I honestly don't know. I've been out of the loop for a while now and haven't really thought about how I'll recruit people."

The women looked out the window at the farmland and rolling hills, and then back at Zaft. "I'm Yora."

Zaft put out his hand to shake. "Zaft, pleasure to meet you."

Yora was a younger than Zaft, at 40. Her brown hair was tied in a bun, and her brown eyes full of youth made him interested. Plus, she wore no wedding ring, which was common for 40-year-olds in this time.

"I have an idea," Yora said. "Why don't you go to an apartment building and figure out how to appear on all the screens in the building. Screens will display you and a small group of people acting out a skit on the sidewalk below. People will recognize where you are and come down. Well, at least some of them will."

"How I am supposed to just show up on their screens?"

"Oh, that part is easy. I work for Soradin and can disrupt internet signals with this little box I carry around. You see, every now and then Soradin needs to inspire people just enough to keep believing in the system. So there are people like me who use the box to play messages to explain how everyone is participating in one global culture by staying on the screen."

Zaft looked perplexed. "And you can just scramble in a video of us doing a skit on the street?"

"Yep… I mean there would be a record of it, and I could get in trouble, but it sounds fun."

"Alright, well, I'll talk to some fellow thespians from my group about this. Can I get your number?" asked Zaft.

"You've already got it," replied Yora. "I can share my number with people just by looking at them and tapping on my middle knuckle three times."

"How convenient!" said Zaft. "What happens if you tap it four times?"

"The plane crashes."

"What?!"

Yora smiled. "You are going to be fun."

Zaft let out a sigh of relief.

They looked down at the comforter of clouds below.

Yora broke the silence. "I heard of this guy, Vic Geraldine, who built antique dollhouses years ago. I think he gave one to Culture Lab. Can you believe that? Dollhouses? Who would ever choose something like that over VR?"

"It wasn't his idea," replied a voice over the intercom.

Everyone in the plane looked up and wondered if the button was pushed while the pilots were talking.

"That was odd," Zaft said. He looked at Yora, then looked back at the blanket of clouds.

In the clouds, Wyoming's face appeared with a smile and a clock tower began to form.

"It can't be," he said.

Yora looked out the window and could not believe her eyes.

Then the face and clock tower disappeared, just like that.

Zaft looked at Yora, eyes wide. "Some years ago, when I first arrived at Culture Lab, that face appeared in my dreams, and in the dreams of many others. Then, after Vic died, he quit showing up."

Yora was almost speechless. "I heard… the rumors… but never believed them. I don't know what to say."

"Don't worry, he wouldn't harm anyone, at least not in a way they could be aware of. It just means he is back to threaten the reversion of humanity to its earliest cultural form."

"Oh, okay." Yora didn't say much for the rest of the plane ride.

# 30

# *Look Behind the Curtain*

By the time the plane landed, Yora had collected her senses.

"So why did he appear to us and no one else," she asked Zaft as they waited for their bags in baggage claim.

"I have a feeling he only appears to certain people," he replied.

"Yeah, that part I got," she said. "But why?"

"Tommy once told us that Wyoming appears to those 'who try to look behind the curtain.'"

"What do you mean?"

"Well, our 'curtain' is what we consider normal in our culture. It's the social rules we follow. Its influenced by our view of reality. A long, long time ago, superstition guided social behavior. People were taught to believe a drought was caused by angry gods, so they prayed and performed rituals to appease the gods. Later on, they performed less dramatic rituals, like wearing their favorite shoes when speaking in public. Now the social rules are strictly loyal to logic. No outside forces intervene, miracles aren't real, luck isn't real, and rituals are useless. Wyoming is looking for people who still yearn for spiritual traditions, who want to look behind the curtain of this era's culture."

Yora made a great counter-argument. "I think our need to belong keeps most people from looking behind the curtain. And I think there is nothing wrong with that."

They both looked at the conveyor belt, wondering why their luggage hadn't come yet. With all the AI integration in society, baggage claim remained sluggish.

Zaft looked back at Yora. "Popular opinion makes people believe their material goods and entertainment preferences indicate their place in the world. Nobody needs to fight the same fight for survival, for recognition, for a special place to live."

"What's wrong with that?" asked Yora.

"I think that's why people are so lonely. They aren't threaded together in a family, community, or string from the past to the future."

"So what?" asked Yora, like a snarky middle schooler.

"Would you look at that, luggage is here," said Zaft in relief.

"You know, you seem like a pretty smart guy," said Yora, trying to recover the connection.

Zaft looked at Yora with a half smile.

Yora grabbed her beige roller bag and Zaft grabbed his gray duffle bag. They walked outside to the car waiting for them.

Zaft was awe-struck by the sight of Derise—an architect's heaven full of buildings shaped like trapezoids, globes, arches, and obtuse triangles. Zero smog as well, as all the earth's power now came from solar and electric. Right as they stepped into their car, Zaft noticed what looked like a hologram talking to someone near the car behind them. He'd heard about the idea of personal hologram buddies as a kid, but didn't believe they'd ever make it out of the movies. He waited to ask Yora about the hologram, waited until he believed that was what it was.

Coincidence had it that Zaft was staying just a few blocks from Yora. So they were dropped off near her apartment, so she could drop her things off, and they could go get coffee. Zaft was to meet the rest of Culture C later that night, so he had some time to kill. At the café, Zaft looked around and could finally take it in that people had personal holograms with them.

Instead of asking Yora, Zaft walked to a person at a café and point-blank asked, "What's with all the holograms?"

The AI-led hologram sitting at the table starting answering the question, but the flesh and bones person interjected.

"Ah, it's another of those resistor-town people. I'll take this one. People have had personal holograms for about ten years or so. Some holograms are actually projections of someone else, like a family member or friend in a different location. This way people can go wherever they want and have access to other people at any time. Other holograms look like new people, but they are run by AI."

"I'm one of those types," said the hologram.

"Interesting. Nice to meet you, I suppose," said Zaft.

Then Zaft looked up and noticed a guy sitting at the edge of the enclosed area in the restaurant's patio. The man stared down at his food and then stared out into the street.

"Thanks," Zaft said to AI hologram and its human companion.

He walked over to the man. "Where is your hologram," he asked, quite directly.

"Well, my wife died three years ago," replied the man.

"I'm sorry to hear that," replied Zaft. He looked at the man, and then looked down at the black asphalt with a mix of confusion and respect.

The man found Zaft's curiosity and courage endearing. "Some of these holograms are people who've died. They are recordings of them. But for me, it never felt right to try to stay connected to Janice by rewatching a recording of her."

"I get that," replied Zaft. After a pause he asked, in an unsure voice. "Is there any way to tell if they are dead or alive?"

"Yes, the hologram's who are dead have a blue line on their hand."

Zaft looked around and saw a few blue lines.

He sat back down with Yora, with a stunned looked on his face.

"Why didn't they have holograms on the plane?" he asked.

"They aren't allowed on the plane, silly. Holograms are only allowed in the departure section of the airport."

"Why?"

"When Soradin first created the technology, people figured out how to completely isolate themselves with their holograms. Behavioral scientists found they were treating holograms like real people. So the government made a rule that you had to leave your house once a week without your hologram. And in situations where there was potential for social interaction, like on an airplane, you needed to turn your hologram off."

"Yeah, but this café has potential for social interaction."

"Yeah, cafés in their first few years of business can opt out of the rule in order to attract customers."

Zaft moved his eyes from table to table, observing the different holograms and their mannerisms. "If you ask me, this is still weird. I mean, look at these people. So sad."

Yora responded directly. "You assume they are sad, but the holograms are convenient. It's relationship on demand, kind of stemming from the principle of entertainment through streaming services in the 21st century." Yora switched topics. "Alright, I am getting hungry. Let's order."

Yora ordered a turkey sandwich with cranberry spread and potato salad side. Zaft ordered a cheeseburger with fries and a cherry soda.

They were both hungry and ate quick. As they neared the end of their meal, Zaft asked Yora, "Can I tell you what I am *really* planning?"

"Yes, do tell!"

"I'd like to teach a broader base of people about the joy of acting."

"Okay, say more."

"That device you have, the one that can interrupt what people watch throughout an apartment building, do you think anyone could build a much bigger one that effects the signal coming from an internet tower?"

Yora sighed. "How about we try to just influence one apartment building's worth of people, and then one city, and then maybe the world? Ya know, one thing at a time?"

"There may not be time," replied Zaft. "Wyoming's appearance earlier indicates the clock is back to ticking."

Yora's enthusiasm for adventure transformed into overwhelm. "I think I've had enough of this craziness today," replied Yora. "You have my number. Call me sometime if you can talk about something else." She left $100 on the table for dinner, got up, and left.

Zaft put his head into his hands. Just then, a waitress walked over.

"Everything okay, sir?"

Zaft looked at her with disappointment. "No. I am afraid we are all going back to cavemen soon."

The waitress had seen plenty of delusional people in the restaurant. People without real friends, or solely AI holograms. People who created alternative realities in their mind to cope with loneliness. She smiled at Zaft. "Well, if we were cavemen, I'd be out in the woods picking berries and connecting with nature. Much better than carrying food to tables and pretending to be interested in people."

Zaft smiled. "Yes, but you'd have to suddenly figure out how to hunt and forage."

"There would be a learning curve," she joked.

Zaft thought, *Maybe all this isn't my responsibility. Maybe I could just blend in and think of culture lab as a just fun adventure in life.*

"Say, what happened to the woman you were with?" asked the waitress.

"I think I scared her off."

"Oh, well, you seem sweet to me. There will be more opportunities."

"Thanks, here is the money for the check. Keep the change."

After the waitress left, he took out a card in his pocket with an apartment address on it: 2304 Bestenshire Lane. This is where he would stay while conducting the Culture Lab experiment with other members from Culture C, who all would be staying in apartments in the same general area he was in. He was supposed to have a group meeting with everyone at a café down the street that afternoon.

When he arrived at his apartment building, it looked like every other apartment building on the block. He used a key card to get inside and went to the place on the third floor. He found a gift basket full of chocolates and personal care items on the mat outside the door. "Welcome to Bestenshire Heights. From your neighbor in apt. 245." Before going in, he put his stuff down and walked over to 245. Before ringing the bell, he noticed a drawing of a cube near the number 245 on a white card slid into a plastic cover on the left side of the door. "*Odd*," he thought.

He rang the bell.

"Just one minute," replied a young man.

Zaft heard some trash get kicked out of the way as the man made his way toward the door.

The door opened. "You must be Zaft! I'm Korch. It's a pleasure to meet you."

"Yeah, likewise, thanks for the gift basket."

"Of course. Would you care to come in for a minute and have some coffee?"

Zaft looked at the him for a minute. Korch was around 20, with black hair, dark brown eyes, and large black eyebrows.

He smiled innocently and waited eagerly like a puppy for Zaft to accept his invitation.

"Ah sure," said Zaft.

The apartment smelled like a college dorm room. Laundry was clearly overdue. The big, egg-white colored couch in the living room had an egg-white colored cat laying on it, and Zaft decided to sit and pet the cat while Korch made coffee. Most of the objects in the living room looked normal: a computer desk, a pizza box, and some hanging posters. But in the corner, Zaft noticed a desk with a 3D printer and a clear glass cube next to it.

"What's with the cube?" Zaft asked candidly.

"That's what you are here to learn about," replied Korch. "I'm just about done with your pour over coffee."

Korch walked over to Zaft, handed him his cup of coffee, and sat down on a big plastic ball on the other side of the coffee table.

"So I've learned Wyoming not only controls the clock tower, but also controls this cube in the universe—this cube produces all the creative energy needed for humanity, and other life forms, to create."

Zaft was about to take his first sip of coffee, but he just held the cup close to his mouth. "How do you know about Wyoming?" he asked.

"I came across some article about him, and about Culture Lab, online. Thought it was crazy at first, then I started researching it more seriously. Then I had a dream with him and this glass cube in it, both in the sky."

After seeing Wyoming on outside the plane window, Zaft had little reason to doubt him.

"Okay, well, he's back," Zaft said.

Korch's eyes grew bigger, and he bobbed up and down on the bouncy ball. "Oh, how wonderful. How marvelous!"

Zaft took his first sip of coffee, which tasted awful, like old beans. Then he asked, rhetorically, "Do you know what will happen to us? I don't think it's wonderful."

Korch knew what Zaft was referring to, but decided not to go there. "My Uncle Arush lived in Culture Lab for some time. He told me all about Wyoming, and…"

"Arush is your uncle?" asked Zaft.

"Yep. He told me about this dream where he learned the dimensions of the cube and the main principle of it. You see, at the center of the cube some sort of energy form unknown to mankind is put under tremendous pressure. And under such pressure creative energy is radiated outward through the universe."

"So you are trying to make a model of the cube on your little 3D printer over there?"

"Yes, exactly, but I can't find the source of energy. I've put rare earth minerals in the middle of the cube. I've learned Tai Chi and have tried to put chi energy in there. I've even tried to capture the energy of depression and put that in there."

"Why would you try depression?"

"Because I think it's a source of creativity," replied Korch. "Plus, there is plenty of it available these days."

"Interesting. How did you get the energy of depression?"

"I have a good friend who is depressed all the time. I asked him to come over, and I put all these nodes on him and attached them to the cube. The nodes picked up his tempera-ture and electrical signals and the cube vibrated as a result."

"How did the cube do that?"

Korch smiled. "I can't tell you all my secrets, but I can tell you I'd like to somehow capture the energy of human connection. I think that could be the secret to creativity."

"I think we can work together," said Zaft. "I am here to teach people acting. There is plenty of connection in that."

# 31

# *Creativity Cube*

"How long do you think it would take you to get five to seven people together for an acting class?" asked Zaft.

Korch thought for a bit. "All my friends are glued to their computers", he said. "It will take a convincing argument to pry them off."

"Can you lie to them and tell them you have some business opportunity you want to meet with them about?"

Korch laughed. "You've spent all those years in Culture Lab. You are finally here to teach society something, and your best plan to get their attention is to tell them you have some business plan?"

"Yes, that's my best plan."

Korch thought about what his friends would really be interested in. He decided to start a group text and tell them a version of the truth. The text read:

"Hey friends. Our city is in trouble. We are constantly on screens for work, games, and social media. We are trapped, even though we feel like we chose this way of life. Join me in doing something different. Meet me today at 5:00 p.m. outside Bestenshire if you want to know more."

"Well, I sent that to almost 30 people. Hopefully seven show up," said Korch.

Zaft smiled. "Good. Let's prepare some improv activities and then write up a script."

"I'll make some coffee," replied Korch.

"Um, do you have tea?"

"Sure."

Zaft stood up and walked to the sliding glass door. He opened it, stood out on the balcony, and admired the park across the street. He admired the holograms and even the stock market numbers projected on the sides of apartment buildings.

"Another year of growth for the tech sector," said Korch, who'd snuck up on him.

"Does it ever go down?" asked Zaft.

"I am not sure. I mean, the numbers never go down, but I wonder who's behind the numbers. Anyway, the market is boring, lets go write our script."

After a few hours of writing together, the two of them produced a poorly written script. "Well it won't ever be up for an award, but it may be good enough," said Korch.

At 4:45 p.m., the first person came to Korch's door. By 5:00 p.m., exactly seven people had arrived.

Korch and Zaft prepared hors d'oeuvres for them to get social and comfortable. Some of them were on the couch, others on the deck. Then Korch called everyone into the living room. He planned to introduce Zaft, but one of the guests kicked everything off.

"So what's the big surprise Korch, are we going to hack into Soradin's network and freeze it?"

"Oh, the opportunity in front of us is much longer lasting," replied Zaft. "Everyone come with me. We are going to walk down to the park across the street."

It was a warm summer day in Derise. A walking path, wooden benches, and oak trees lined the perimeter of the half-acre grass park across the street from the apartment building.

The group circled the grass while Korch came around with the cube. It didn't look special. Just a clear plastic cube with a pocket of air. Korch held it up. "This cube may have the ability to pick up the energy of connection and turn it into pure creative energy."

Some members of the group snickered. "Could it clean my toilet, too?"

Korch chucked. "Yes, it sounds crazy, but I am just going to set this cube down on the bench behind everyone, and you don't have to think about it anymore. We are just going to listen to Zaft, and we'll see what the cube does."

Zaft stepped into the middle of the circle.

"Okay, this game is called Know Your Roll. In this game, you are going to pick someone in society to emulate. It could be a teacher, a president, an AI hologram, whatever. Whoever you pick, attach a status to your character, low or high. Then, when we are done, we are all going to assume character and simply walk around this area of grass. The point is to see the importance of contrast when characters relate to each other."

"Wait, is this an acting class?" asked someone. "I thought those went out of style like fifty years ago."

All the other adults looked excited to go on with the game.

"Now pick your character and status," said Zaft, "but don't tell any of us."

People began walking around the grass, passing each other with chests pointed out, or head drooped toward compressed shoulders.

"Now I want you to pick a partner and get into a conversation while in your role. At the end, your partner will try to guess who you are."

Everyone paired up, but then got silent.

"We don't know what to say," one of them said. "We've never done anything like this."

After enough time in his social experiment, Zaft had forgotten people in public didn't really talk to each other about anything. Technology offered all the answers to daily questions and most relationships, including friendships, were started and maintained online. People talked at work, but only during company structured "talk time."

"People only talk with their close family," said one of the participants.

Zaft sighed. "Okay, lets circle up again. This time I want you to pretend your sibling is coming from out of town to stay with you for three days. I want you to pretend they have been at your place for five days. You need to have a conversation with them about leaving, but it will be difficult.

"Um, do we have to do this?" asked a group member. "It's just so awkward."

Just then, Tommy walked up to the group. "Oooh, can I play the brother they are going to kick out?"

"Tommy, hey, um, what are you doing here?"

"Oh just checking in on the world-saving status of my groups. Zaft, have you checked in with other members from Culture C Group yet?"

"Um not yet," replied Zaft. He knew it was past the time they'd agreed to meet. "I met this guy, Korch, who may have some additional information on Wyoming that you may find useful. Maybe if you just hang out for a bit, I can set up something for the group and you and I can talk."

"Sure," Tommy said.

Zaft directed his attention back to the group. "I know this is a bit awkward, but just keep in mind conversations don't always play out like a beautiful piece of music. Sometimes a string breaks. If we avoid those moments, we avoid real closeness. That being said, improv skits are hard, so I'll give you all twenty minutes to come up with something. Shoot for a two- to three-minute skit. Again, the goal is to pretend you have a sibling over-staying their welcome in your home."

The groups paired up into even teams, since Korch made the group eight instead of seven.

Zaft and Tommy walked over to a park bench to talk.

Zaft went on with his story. "When I got to my room there was this gift basket from this young guy down the hall. I knocked on his door and he invited me in. I worried about being too trusting, but something about him said it would be okay. Anyway, he showed me this plastic cube he made with a 3D printer and he said he knew about Wyoming."

"Did he say what the cube was for?" asked Tommy, with curiosity in his face.

"Yeah, I guess Wyoming operates this cube in the universe that's the source of all creativity. The cube hasn't been working well since the global population transitioned to working alone on computers all day. So Korch wondered if he could build a miniature creativity cube, one to capture different energies, like Chi, and even depression, and then turn that into creative energy. Now we are trying to see if the cube will capture the energy of connection."

"Ah, great idea," said Tommy. "Proud of you for being willing to divert from the original plan."

"Well, it's about showtime," said Zaft. "Let's go check in on the cube and our actors." The groups were excited and nervous to perform.

The first group kept it simple:

"What do you mean it's time to go? I'm your brother."

"Listen, this isn't about you specifically. We love you. We just need our space."

Another group was much more descriptive and animated:

"You know going home is returning to hell. My husband is constantly criticizing everything I do. It's so toxic there. I can never go back."

"Why don't you just leave him?"

"I could ask you the same thing about your husband."

"Okay, that's enough. Get your stuff and go."

"Okay, fine." [actor sulks as they walk away].

"Wait, come here. It was my husband's idea to ask you to leave, but he didn't have the courage. I'll talk to him. Come, give me a hug."

At this point in the show, everyone heard a hum from the cube on the bench, which also radiated soft white light, like a lamp.

Instantaneously, the group stood on a glass floor inside a larger glass cube, floating out in space. Somehow there was light, even though they were far from any stars.

"What the?"

"I think I am ready for the game to be over Korch. Get us out of the virtual simulation."

Korch smiled. "I didn't think it would work. I thought at most we'd be able to see something different in the little cube. I didn't think we'd get transported to the great cube. We should be smooshed by the pressure in the middle of this thing."

Another period of silence passed.

"The great cube?" asked someone.

"Welcome!" Wyoming's deep, low voice rattled the glass around them. He walked out of one glass side and walked over to the group. He wore a black suit and dress shoes, as if he needed the authority. With a chiseled face and thick black hair, Wyoming looked like a model. Maybe he just took this form as a demigod knowing humans mistakenly found more attractive people to be more believable.

"You're here, you made it," Wyoming said with a smile. "This machine allows you humans, and other creatures in the universe, to create. This machine gave the earliest humans the idea for fire, and later humans the idea of flight."

Zaft turned his body 360 degrees. "There is no pressure on me. How is this machine working?"

"Ah yes. The mechanics of it. Just keep going with your skit. That'll make everything appear to you," replied Wyoming.

The actors looked at each other. They didn't have much choice.

"I guess if we keep going with it, more will be revealed," said one of them.

They found their partners and resumed their roles.

"What if I told *you* I was coming to your house for three days and stayed for five?"

"I would let you stay as long as you'd like."

"Sure. Right. Let's try it sometime. When you and my wife try to have a conversation, all I hear is nails on the chalkboard."

Blue, green, purple and yellow lights shot through the walls of the cube, like lighting. The actors kept acting. Their skits became more and more original.

"This is about the time mom and dad told me my ambitions were so big, I could pick any star in the sky as my own. And yet they told you, dear brother, to pick the first job you got out of college. You want my life, and you can't have it, no matter how long you stay here."

"Maybe that's true. Maybe you're right. I can't make my life as good as yours, no matter how hard I try."

"I'm sorry I said that. The truth is my life isn't all it's cracked up to be."

The two actors hugged each other, and then separated and looked at the group. Not knowing how to end their skit one of them just said, "We're done."

The group clapped. One of the actors turned to Wyoming.

One of them spoke up. "I feel like blood is running through my veins again."

Wyoming had a satisfied look on his face, as if he just finished the last bite of a delicious meal. "Good," he said. "This is the experience of unearthing human needs buried by your modern culture. Earth's one global culture isn't created by a need for meaning or connection. It helps you get what you physically need, and it keeps you stimulated, but it's lonely. Your lack of connection also blurs memory and keeps the mind running on a separate track from the body. You may think you are connected with snippets, or posts, online. These are just morsels of belonging frozen in time, never sufficient enough to create lasting memories."

Tommy looked at Zaft. "Couldn't have said it better myself."

"You are all ordinary people selected for an extraordinary job," said Wyoming. "When you go back to earth, you'll each get a tool from this machine to take with you. Your tool will inspire others."

"People don't want toys," said one of actors. "Don't you know the whole world discarded their toys fifty years ago?"

"People just need more support in rediscovering their playful side," replied Tommy. "It's natural to be scared to lose one's sense of belonging that comes from conforming. It's natural to be scared of criticism for making room for play in life."

"So I want each one of you to reach into one of the glass walls and pull out a tool," Wyoming said.

The colorful intersecting lines in the cube had diminished. The crew stood on one side of the cube and looked at Wyoming. They wondered if there was a trick up his sleeve. Maybe each one of them would get teleported to a different galaxy upon reaching into the glass wall of the cube.

With courage, Tommy approached one of the walls. Everyone looked at him nervously as he reached his hand in. He pulled out a shiny ball, the size of a golf ball.

"Ah the Stellevolk Orb. That's a good one," said Wyoming. "If an adult looks at it, a uniquely interesting toy will appear in front of them. It may be a toy from a century before, or many centuries before. But whatever it is, your subject will not be able to control their fascination with it."

Then Zaft walked to the wall and put his hand in. Out came a metal triangle with a string tied to it.

"Don't forget the mallet," said Wyoming.

Zaft reached back in and pulled out a shiny green mallet.

"I've seen one of these triangle instruments in a museum," he said. "I think they just make one tone."

"Ah but this one is different, give it a try," replied Wyoming.

Zaft hit it and the sound of a harmonizing choir came out. The sound contained baritone voices, making everyone feel a warmth in their core, and soprano voices that sang like an American goldfinch. Those soprano tones gave the group a feeling of joy like seeing a happy baby.

"Now hit the triangle in a new place," said Wyoming.

Zaft hit the triangle on the other side, and a symphony played. "Where is the sound coming from?" he asked.

"Wouldn't you love to know!" exclaimed Wyoming. "Just show people what it can do. It will spark a flame."

Just then Vic, who had been gone from Earth for years now, walked through the glass. He wore tan corduroy pants, a blue and green flannel shirt, and a fedora cap. He was holding a dollhouse.

"Vic?" exclaimed Tommy. Vic smiled and put down the dollhouse. Then Tommy ran over and gave him a hug, like a ten-year-old giving his grandpa a hug.

"Yep, it's me. Good to see you, Tommy. Ya know, being able to go anywhere in space within seconds is pretty awesome. Somehow, I sensed you found the cube."

They released each other and Tommy put his hand on his waist. "You look exactly the same as you did on earth. You always wore that outfit."

Vic smiled. "Creature of habit, I guess. Well, spirit of habit now. You look similar to the ten-year-old kid I once knew. Much taller now. I hope you kept your sense of adventure over these years."

"Oh don't worry about that Vic. By the way, I still have that Chinese Dollhouse you gave me."

"Ah yes, the one with neat garden and coy pond in the middle. If you think that is cool, check out this one. Vic picked up the dollhouse at his feet. This dollhouse was actually my grandmother's. You can tell by the planes she drew on the walls of a kid's room."

Vic pointed at the room and everyone in the cube, even Wyoming, moved in closer to get a look.

"I've since made a few modifications," Vic said. "Most importantly, this dollhouse will write scripts based on scenes kids and adults create. So imagine a mother and her daughter playing together, creating some kind of scene with their dolls. They can put the dollhouse into record mode, and not only will it copy their dialogue, it will make notes on the dollhouse room they are in, and the emotions presented. The script then gets printed out of the back of the dollhouse. This way, families can write short plays without overthinking it, and they can have a script to use to perform the play again, or to have as a keepsake."

Although his greatest legacy survived in the memories of Sonata, Gale, and Tommy, Vic still enjoyed the sense of completion in his unanticipated, unconventional, dollhouse-making journey.

"So what exactly are we supposed to do with all these toys?" asked Zaft.

"Make memories," replied Wyoming.

"Oh, I don't think people will struggle to remember these," commented Korch.

"You'd be surprised how quickly a novel idea is forgotten," replied Wyoming. "Your task is to make people care more about making memories than they do about being entertained or getting validation online."

The people in the group went silent. The only sound remaining came from a steady hum in the cube's walls. Instantly, a cardboard box appeared in the middle of cube.

"That's to put your toys in," said Wyoming. "Goodbye."

Suddenly, the group was back in the park. It took them a minute to regain full alertness. On a bench nearby, a man sat up and rubbed his forehead. He vaguely remembered dreaming about a glass cube out in the middle of space.

**32**

# *On with the Play!*

The man on the bench had little recollection of who he was. But he saw a group of people sitting on a blanket in the grass and thought he'd ask them. "Excuse me, do any of you know who I am?" The group looked at the man with jaws dropped.

"Wyoming?"

"Is that my name?"

Tommy looked at everyone in the circle. "I'll explain," he said.

"Yes, your name is Wyoming. Now what I am going to tell you may sound very strange, but just bear with me. You worked in accounting at Soradin a number of years ago, but you went missing. You turned into a spiritual being, and that being warned humanity of being reset to cavemen if they didn't do something to restore a sense of connectedness and imagination. You may have been this being all along because everyone has a spiritual nature but many of us lose connection with it. The world's demands on our attention can cause our soul to hide away, like a child in a closet. So, you went on a great journey to inspire people, and now you are back."

Wyoming had many questions, but the most important one sifted to the top of his mind. "I'm hungry, where can I get food?"

The group laughed. "There is a pizza place right across the street. I'll join you and we'll get pizza for everyone," said Tommy.

On the way over, Wyoming asked Tommy, "What do I do now? Do I have to go back to my life as it was?"

"That's up to you. We are here in the park to have fun with all the cool toys you gave us in the other dimension we were all in just a minute ago. Maybe you can just spend the day with us and worry about what you'll do with your life tomorrow."

"Sure," said Wyoming. He put aside his need to figure things out for a just a bit.

Back at the park, they brainstormed. "We could start with presentations at elementary schools," proposed Zaft.

Korch chuckled. "I can imagine the pitch email to the school principle: 'Hi, we are a group of entertainers looking to create lasting memories in kids. We have some fun toys to help with this, such as a speakerless metal triangle that plays a symphony through it.'"

"How about we just tell them we are an acting troupe, and we present the triangle by surprise?" asked Zaft. "Live plays havn't been done in years, so the idea of bringing them back could possibly be enticing to a school."

"Good idea. What would the play be about?" asked Korch.

"Why don't we just recreate the experience in the cube. An acting group gets transported into space and picks up all these magical toys to bring back to earth."

"Right, and then we get some kids to volunteer to try them out," said Korch.

"And make them faint?" asked one of the volunteers.

The group saw Tommy and Wyoming walking back, smiling. They were reminiscing on the mall experience, where they dressed up as pirates, saw into the future, and witnessed a spirit of some kind raise the mall's glass ceiling into a dome.

"Pizza will be ready in 45 minutes," said Wyoming. He noticed a woman walking toward the group. "Is she with you all?" he asked.

"Yep, that's my new girlfriend," said Tommy. "Her name is Leila." She walked over and didn't really seem to notice anyone else but Tommy.

She gave him a hug and kiss. "Hey sweetie, I got off work a bit early to come see what you were up to." The group looked confused, as Tommy never had a girlfriend at Culture Lab.

Tommy picked up on their confusion. "We met a two months ago online."

"Now I have to be honest and say we released you all into *this* city for a few reasons."

As Leila told the group about herself, Sonata arrived, making for quite a lively afternoon. Sonata smiled when she saw Tommy had a girlfriend, but before she could ask Leila any questions, Tommy said, "You would not believe where we've been."

"Oh I don't know, maybe some glass cube floating out in space?" replied Sonata, in her precocious thirteen-year-old tone.

"How did you know?" said Zaft.

She put her hands in his tan khakis and smiled. "Wyoming was in my dream last night, standing in the glass cube." The group remained silent, contemplating why Wyoming wanted Sonata to know about the cube.

"Don't look at me," Wyoming said. "I've got no memory of that other guy."

Sonata went on. "I see you got some new toys, and I see you got my dad's dollhouse there."

"Well, it's got some modifications," said Tommy. He looked at Zaft, grabbed two puppets, and gave Zaft one of them. Since they had the model of Vic's grandmother's dollhouse, the skit took place on a farm in the 20th century. Tommy started acting as a mother in the skit, just because. "You go put some water on the stove. I'll go dust the upstairs really quick, because heaven knows it sure needs it. After tea, we'll go feed the horses and drive a few more posts in on the fence."

"Mom," said Zaft, pretending to be the son in the skit, "can we do everything but drive more posts in? I hate digging post holes."

"If you can dig two post holes today, I'll give you two scoops of ice cream."

The two waited and the dollhouse printed their script with the scene details of "farm house, middle 20th century."

"Wow, we barely gave it any information and it concluded we were in the 20th century? It's like reading my imagination or something," said Zaft.

Sonata smiled and a tear rolled down her cheek. "That's why Dad wanted to make all those dollhouses to begin with. The dollhouse made him feel cherished for his imagination.

He lived a useful life as a therapist, no doubt, but he always gave practical advice and never reached into the world of fiction to help his patients. Yet he read stories to me all the time. He read stories about spirit foxes from the Native American mythology, and spirit chickens from African mythology. He read stories that taught me about the world through imagination."

"Lets write a play about him, shall we?" replied Tommy.

Sonata wiped her tears away. "Who, Vic?"

"Yes, Vic, he's sorta the Godfather of this whole culture-change enterprise we are running."

"Okay, what kind of dolls are in here anyway?" she asked as she put her hand in the toybox. She pulled out a stubby doll with corduroys, a red flannel shirt, and a bald head.

"That's strange," she said. "Guess we got a mini Vic now. Hey Dad, if this is you, wink at me," she joked. She gave the doll about ten seconds, but no wink.

"On with the play!" demanded Korch.

"Okay, friends, let us begin," announced Zaft. "Tommy, will you grab your doll? Everyone else, grab a doll or a toy, let's play." As some of the group went on with the play, others grabbed toys from the box. A woman in the group grabbed the Stellevolk Orb and started walking around the perimeter of the park with it. Each person she passed looked at the Orb and a toy they'd always wanted appeared. So along the trail appeared a little carousal, a red wagon, a space fighter lego set, and many things people of this era had never even seen. But somehow it was in their imagination.

Meanwhile, a man with a triangle walked around and Chopin's Nocturnes played throughout the park. At this time in the afternoon, people living in Bestenshire Place, nearly all of them, walked on their treadmills while working on computers. They began to sense something happening in the park. They removed their headphones and walked toward their windows. The park was filled with magical toys and music and actors. Curiosity grew like a spider plant on the window sill. And somewhere out there in the universe, a being that no longer looked human kept the Culture Clock stopped and the glass cube humming.

THE END

# *About the Author*

Being orphaned and adopted at seven, Bo always yearned for what he thought was a normal family. But, instead of grasping for the impossible, he came to appreciate all the people who stepped in to raise him and he began to embrace humanity as his family. Now living in Bellingham, WA, Bo writes about opportunities to find connection and meaning in a confusing and technology-dominated world. He is also a musician and music teacher, which connects him to family members he wishes were still with us. With the help of many others, Bo runs a non-profit called Gifts of Music NW, which brings music education to people who face various barriers.